FIREPOWER
A Four Corners Thriller

Cryptic Bindings
Seattle

MIKE ATTEBERY

FIRE POWER

A **FOUR CORNERS** THRILLER

FIREPOWER
A Four Corners Thriller

www.mikeattebery.com

First Edition: April 2019

ISBN: 978-1-7337394-0-5

**For
Steph and Charley**

STATE ROAD 170
FARMINGTON, NEW MEXICO

For ten-year-old Bryan Myers, the highlight of his family's frequent summer road trips was scouring the comic book spinners at the rest stops when they pulled off the highway to refuel. Remote convenience stores and trading posts often held exceptional finds, back issues of comics with characters and story arcs he had never heard of before. Over the course of the family's travels this summer, Bryan had found a complete set of *Damage Control* comics from the late-80s, as well as a bundle of *Spider-Man* titles in which Spidey was sporting some sort of all-black, alien costume. How these issues had managed to stay tucked away in the spinners all these years was a mystery, but there they sat, suspended in time, just waiting for Bryan's discovery. Amazingly, most of the stores were still honoring the original cover prices as well, some of them as low as 60 cents!

While reluctant to embark on another long drive in the blistering heat, the prospect of unearthing further treasures was enough to get Bryan to join his older brother in the back of the family's motorhome without complaint. Knowing the reason behind their younger son's willingness to embark on another impromptu excursion, Ray and Diane Myers made a point of stopping at the first trading post on the outskirts of town to give Bryan a chance to pick up more comics, and grab some candy for he and his brother.

After weighing his options – settling on a handful of *Wolverines* and two bargain-priced, yet satisfyingly-heavy *Big Hunk* bars – Bryan paid the cashier and walked out of the Truax Trading Post, clutching his prizes as he crossed the dirt parking lot en route to the family's glistening RV.

"What did you get me?" Jason called out the window as his younger brother approached.

Bryan held up the king-sized nougat bars for inspection.

Jason nodded in approval. "Not bad."

Bryan pulled the door open and was just climbing up the steps, when the sound of squealing tires filled the air. He spun around to see a bright orange Chevette come tearing down the highway past the parking lot. Flickering flames filled the car's interior, reminding him of the front of Stephen King's *Firestarter,* which Jason had been reading all summer. No sooner did the book cover pop into his mind, then the speeding vehicle swerved out of control, slamming into a ditch on the far side of the road. The driver's side door flew open, and a figure emerged from the vehicle, fully engulfed in flames.

"Oh my God!" Ray shouted as he ran to grab the fire extinguisher from the back of the motorhome.

Diane looked on in shock, before hurrying over to cover Bryan's eyes.

"Boys!" She screamed. "Don't look!"

"Why not?" Jason asked incredulously.

Bryan reached up and pried his mother's fingers out of the way. The driver resembled the Human Torch from *The Fantastic Four,* at least for a moment, before the flames overtook him, and he disappeared into a thick black cloud of burning fabric and flesh. A guttural howl rippled through the air as the man writhed and flailed about in the flames.

Ray ran along the side of the road, looking for oncoming cars before he crossed the scorching hot blacktop. Even as he watched his father closing the distance, Bryan could see it was no use. After the first staggered steps, the burning man fell silent as he dropped to his knees, tumbled forward, and lay still.

Smoke and steam billowed under the blast of the extinguisher, as Ray swept the spray back and forth over the flames. But it was too late, the driver's twisted body lay sprawled out on the sizzling ground, burned and contorted beyond all recognition, one arm reaching out for the help that could never have gotten to him in time.

Ray looked over at his wife and shook his head.

Diane took Bryan and Jason into the trading post to call the police.

High above the scene, lost in the blinding glare of the sun, a lone vulture circled overhead, watching the figures down below, waiting for the body to cool.

1.

"ALL IN ALL, I'D say I've done a pretty good job for the people of Farmington," Tim Givens said.

"Just 'pretty good,' councilman?" Luke Murphy asked as he flipped to a fresh page in his notebook. At 34 years of age, Luke was still boyishly handsome, with a head of uncombed, salt and pepper hair, which had taken on a touch more salt than pepper over the last year. "Any accomplishments you'd be especially inclined to highlight for our readers?"

Councilman Givens dug into his Frito pie – the Five and Dime's signature combination of crispy corn chips, chili, and grated cheddar cheese – crunching on a mouthful as he chewed the question over. He was in his early 50s, sporting a head of slicked-back black hair, with touches of white at the temples. Luke knew from previous election-year profiles that Givens had entered city government after a long career in the oil and gas business, where he'd worked his way up from field work to the executive level.

As far as Luke could tell, the years wore easy on Givens. Decades of sun exposure had etched only the gentlest of lines down his tanned face, subtle crow's feet lingered at the corners of his hazel eyes. Subsequent decades of easy living had no doubt smoothed away the rougher edges, leaving the councilman with a generally relaxed disposition, evident as he raised a laconic finger to flag their waitress down for a coffee refill. Yet now and then throughout the interview, the councilman would rock forward, banging a fist on the table in their booth, betraying a wound-up intensity that had no doubt served him well professionally over the years.

Givens had been on the city council for the better part of a decade, and his re-election was practically a given, but that didn't mean he could skip the formalities of a campaign. He still needed to make the rounds about town, pressing the flesh, appearing on the more parochial local television programs, and submitting to interviews like this one for the newspaper. Luke had interviewed the councilman many times before and considered him a likable and talented politician. It wouldn't have surprised him to learn that Tim Givens had greater political ambitions, perhaps a run for mayor might be in his future, but for now, his sights seemed set on re-election and finishing his Frito pie.

"Look, you know the background I bring to the council," Givens said. "The energy industry knows they can always come to me when they need a knowledgeable, *experienced* voice in city government, and in turn, no one has done more to bring work back to the Four Corners, save for Ben Gerritt, and we all know how that turned out. You better than anyone."

Luke nodded, ready to move on to another question. Givens was referring to the story he had broken the previous year, a scandal involving one of the city's elder statesmen, and a history of political corruption that Farmington would be struggling to get past for a long time to come.

"That may be my greatest selling point," The councilman continued, "Out of everyone on the council, I'm the only one who never had any dealings, professional or political, with Ben Gerritt. My record is clean."

"Speaking of clean, and circling back to your energy background, the council's big solar vote is tonight. Anything you'd like to say about that?"

"The solar farm?" Givens cracked a wide grin. "I think my position is well known on that front. Alternative energy is a cute idea, wind and sunshine solving our energy challenges is an entertaining fairy tale, but it's just that, a wistful fantasy. There are no free lunches, my friend. The upfront costs are astronomical, and I just don't see it penciling out in the end. Alan Greenwood can spend his money as he sees fit, but I believe Farmington should steer clear."

"It's brought a lot of construction jobs to the region already. That's been a good thing, correct?"

"True, but if this plant is such a boon for the city in the long term, why is Greenwood trying to offload a chunk of the completion expenses this late in the process?"

"That I can't answer," Luke replied. He'd never met Greenwood, but the man had a reputation as a bit of an opaque eccentric, albeit, an eccentric who had amassed a staggering fortune over the course of his long and varied career. "Should I assume you're a 'no' then?'"

The councilman took a long sip of his coffee. "When will this profile run?"

"Sometime next week I expect."

Givens' eyes glimmered as he set his mug down and leaned back in his seat. "You'll have to come to the meeting tonight and find out," he said.

Luke smiled. Spoken like a true politician. Whatever his final vote, Tim Givens didn't want it noted in the media push for his re-election, no doubt hoping to attract voters with dogs on either side of the fight, and hoping readers with conflicting loyalties would fail to put the pieces together on their own.

Betty, an older woman with a blue beehive hairdo, came by their booth with their receipt. She had always been Luke's favorite waitress at the Five and Dime.

"I can ring the two of you out if you're all set," Betty said as she added up their tab. "I hope everything was satisfactory."

"Excellent!"

"As good as ever," Luke echoed.

"Councilman, did you know this young man has been coming in here since he was eight years old?"

"Is that right?"

"Mike Murphy's boy," Betty continued. "All grown up." She set the bill between the two of them, giving Luke a subtle wink as she nudged it closer to Givens on the off-chance he was paying for the meal.

"Thanks, Betty," Luke said as he quickly leaned forward to grab the check. "This one is on *The Times*."

Betty walked away and Luke turned to his briefcase on the seat beside him. He set his thumbs on the well-worn clasps, only one of which still closed, and popped the top open. The only things inside were a laptop computer, a bag of marshmallow circus peanuts, a rubber-banded bundle of business cards, and a Visa from the paper. He pulled out the credit card and closed the briefcase, latching the functioning clasp before he got up.

"Aren't they paying you enough over there to pick up a decent bag?" Givens asked.

"It was my Dad's. It's beat up, but it gets the job done," Luke said. "If I didn't have the computer, I'd probably just carry my notebook and a golf pencil."

"Still, I'd be afraid the thing would pop open," the councilman said as he pointed to the one working clasp.

Luke shrugged. "Worst-case scenario, the laptop breaks and I'm back to just my notebook, the way I like it."

"You're sort of a luddite, aren't you?"

"And proud of it," Luke said as he walked to the register to pay Betty for their lunch.

"For a politician, he's pretty cute," Betty said with a wink as she watched Givens getting out of the booth. "I like his type."

Luke laughed. "Aren't you married?"

"Forty-five years, but a girl can dream, Luke. A girl can dream"

She slid the receipt across the counter as Givens approached.

Luke took five dollars from his back pocket and dropped it in the tip jar. "I'll see you next time."

"Councilman," Betty said with a smile.

"Have a good afternoon, ma'am," Givens replied as he took a toothpick from the dispenser next to the register.

"Thank you for your time," Luke said to the councilman as they stepped outside.

"I appreciate it." Givens reached out and squeezed Luke's hand. "Will I see you at tonight's vote?"

"You can count on it."

Luke tucked his notebook into his back pocket and surveyed the Mesa Shopping Center's sizzling parking lot as Givens headed for his car. The temperature had been broiling when he first arrived, but now that the summer sun was at its peak, the mercury was climbing into *Looney Tunes* exploding-thermometer territory. He was loath to head back to *The Daily Times* offices, but at least the air conditioning would be a welcome change of pace.

Despite a recent rebuild, Luke's black '68 Mustang was already looking just as weathered as it had before a work-related mishap the previous year had necessitated a complete bumper to bumper overhaul. The driver's side door groaned irritably as Luke pulled on the handle, releasing a cloud of hot air as it swung open. He climbed in and started the engine, rotating the scorching hot steering wheel with the palms of his hands as he headed downtown.

2.

RED AND BLUE LIGHTS whirled atop the dusty squad cars parked along the side of the road, the sweep of their beams largely washed out in the glare of the afternoon sun. A uniformed officer directed the sparse traffic driving past the scene. The medical examiner's refrigerated van was parked at the back of the lineup of police cars, the air conditioning pulling in a predictable crowd as detective Alex Spencer arrived at the scene. With sun-streaked brown hair that fell just past her chin, Alex cut an unusual figure for a Farmington police officer. Overlooking the fact that she was a woman in a club of mostly men, at 27, she was also the youngest member of the force to ever hold the title of detective. She had only recently relocated to Farmington, coming from Albuquerque's much larger police department. Individually, any of these credentials would have drawn attention, but combined, they'd earned her the type of scrutiny usually reserved for known criminals, not attractive young police officers.

She parked at the back of the lineup of cars, already anticipating the sidelong glances from her fellow officers. The department was in flux after a much-publicized scandal the previous year, one which had rocked the force and drawn statewide scrutiny. The subsequent shakeup had opened up a lot of jobs across all levels of law enforcement. That was the primary reason she'd made the leap to the Four Corners region. Despite a stellar if brief tenure, it would have been *years* before she'd have had a shot at detective if she'd stayed in Albuquerque. Yet, it was a job she was well suited for, and she was quickly hired for the position in Farmington. Unfortunately, although the changes had been sweeping, and the house-cleaning thorough, an underlying level of mistrust remained in the department, even amongst the new hires. It felt as though they were all keeping an eye on her to see if she could be trusted. Alex was also well aware of the unfortunate fate that had befallen her predecessor, and though she told herself the corrupt forces which had brought about his demise had been ferreted out and dealt with, it seemed wise to keep her defenses up for the foreseeable future. Just in case.

She nodded at a few familiar faces as she walked toward the center of the action. Yellow tape blocked off a section of roadway, where a sheet of white plastic was draped over the unmistakable shape of a body stretched out across the blacktop. A burned boot stuck out from the closest corner. A compact orange car, dating back to at least the 70s, had run into a ditch on the side of the road, coming to rest at such an extreme angle that the front passenger side tire was lifted up off the ground. The driver side door was open, and through it Alex could see an open briefcase sitting on the passenger seat. The outside of the case was tanned leather, the inside looked scorched and blackened.

Alex turned at the sound of a camera shutter to her right, and saw Jim Burgess, the department's bearded crime scene photographer, crouching down to get a shot of the vehicle.

"Hi Jim," she said.

"Fancy meeting you here," Burgess replied, the stick from a lollipop jutting out of the corner of his mouth. He was one of the good guys, and had been on the police payroll for the better part of thirty years. In that time, he'd seen any number of grotesqueries, it would take a lot more than the sight of a flambéed motorist to keep him from his signature watermelon Dum-dums.

"You shot the victim yet?"

"Yep." He nodded. "Face, hands, full body, every angle, nook, and cranny. This guy died *badly*. Burned alive."

"Intentional you think?"

"Someone's intent, but probably not his." he pointed over his shoulder at the attaché that had caught Alex's eye as she walked up. "If I had to guess, I'd say there was something planted in that briefcase."

Alex looked around the crowd. "Who's handling the scene?"

"John Knudsen," Burgess said, pointing to an older guy with a white crewcut and mirrored sunglasses.

"I haven't worked with him yet. Anything I should know?"

"He's OK. Old timer. Kind of a hard-ass, but as honest as the day is long. I worked a few scenes with him back in the nineties. Guess they pulled him out of mothballs while things are in transition."

Alex watched Knudsen talking to the other officers. He was a big guy, with a solid frame and a wide stance. He struck her as a drill sergeant type, barking out orders with a poker face, his eyes hidden behind reflective lenses. The white hair and a slight hunch were the only hints that he was even *eligible* for retirement, let alone that he'd been pulled off the bench to rehabilitate the department.

"Sergeant?" she asked Burgess before she walked over.

He shook his head. "Captain."

She nodded her thanks and raised the yellow tape to duck under.

"Captain Knudsen," Alex said as she approached.

He pivoted on one foot and looked at her blankly.

"Alex Spencer."

"Ah, detective." He said as he gave her the once over. "Glad you could join us."

"What do we know so far?" Alex asked, ignoring the dig.

"In broad strokes? This guy came tearing around the bend like a bat out of hell, swerved off the road, and emerged from the vehicle engulfed in flames. Smoke and fire got the better of him, and he dropped dead in the middle of the road."

"Who saw it happen?"

Knudsen pointed to a family sitting on a picnic bench across the street. "The husband tried to save the guy. He put the fire out with an extinguisher, but the poor bastard was a cinder by the time he got to him."

Alex looked over at the husband and wife and their two sons. She'd get a full statement from them in a moment.

"Do we have an ID on the deceased?"

"Not yet," Knudsen said as he led her over to the vehicle. "The car is a rental, but we haven't found any paperwork. If he had the agreement on him, it must have been in one of his pockets, along with his wallet and ID."

Alex peered in through the driver's door, surveying the seats and dash. The car was dated, but well-maintained.

"Looks like an oldie but a goody," she noted.

"Chevette," Knudsen said, slapping his hand on the roof. "They're *still* better than half the cars on the road."

A rail-thin, white-haired officer to his right chuckled. He looked to be in his late-50s Another callback from the bench of retirees, Alex figured.

"The hell you laughing at, Peterson?" Knudsen barked.

Mike Peterson smiled at Alex as he pointed one thumb Knudsen's way. "The captain here had one of these jalopies twenty-five years ago. Even *then,* he was trying to pass them off as hot rods instead of roller skates."

"They're good machines," Knudsen retorted. "Solid!"

"Eventually, even *shit* turns solid, Captain."

Knudsen took a slow, deep breath. "Peterson here likes to get me riled up, but as I was saying, they're reliable vehicles, and this one seems to be in extremely good shape."

"Kind of outdated for a rental car, don't you think?"

"You know how it is," Knudsen said. "You get out to Taos or up into southern Colorado, you start dealing with some unconventional business owners. At least this one appreciates the classics."

"Any theories on the fire?" Alex asked. "It seems to have torched the driver, but spared everything else"

"Yeah, we've been puzzling over that," Knudsen said. "I'd see what your lab guy makes of the briefcase on the passenger seat. If I had to guess, I'd say something in there went boom."

"Something the driver was transporting, or something that was planted?"

"How the hell should I know? Maybe someone slipped an explosive into this guy's bag, maybe he was on his way to Farmington Lake to go fishing with dynamite-"

"Nah-" Peterson interjected.

"What?" Knudsen snapped, annoyed at the interruption.

"It definitely wasn't dynamite. That would have blown the roof and doors off. This was incendiary, not explosive…"

"I don't give a shit what it was," Knudsen noted as he headed back to the body. "Just as long as it doesn't take me another three hours to clear this crime scene."

Alex crossed the road to the trading post parking lot, where the Myers family was having ice cream.

"Thank you for your patience, folks," she said as she approached. "I'm sure you have other places you'd rather be right now."

"Not really," the youngest boy chimed in. "They're giving us free ice cream and comics. I could stay here all day!"

"Oh really?" Alex smiled. "Well that's good to hear…"

"Bryan," the boy replied.

"That's good to hear, Bryan. But I'm sure your parents are anxious to get going."

"We're glad to help if we can," his mother said. "I'm Diane, this is Ray."

"I'm Detective Spencer," Alex said as she shook their hands. "Ray, you were filling your gas tank when the car approached?"

"That's right."

"And, after it slid off the road, did you see the moment of… ignition?"

"Not exactly. Whatever went wrong, it must have happened just before I saw him. There were flames inside the car as he drove past, like he was already on fire."

"Oh really?" Alex said, taking note of the timing. "Well, that likely negates my next question, but can you give me any sort of description of the driver?"

"Between the flames and the glare off the windshield, I couldn't see much of anything for certain."

"Such an awful way to go!" Diane exclaimed.

Alex had to agree. As far as bad deaths went, this was now at the top of her list.

"What about the fire? Was it just on his clothing? Was it all over?"

"He was *engulfed*," Ray said.

"Any sort of smell? Like fuel or chemicals or anything like that?"

"Yeah, but I can't quite put my finger on it. Did you smell it?" Ray asked his wife.

"Thankfully, no."

"It smelled liked my G.I. Joe when Jason burned it with Dad's lighter," Bryan noted.

Diane's head shot up. "When he did *what?*"

"Bryan, quit making stuff up!" Jason shouted.

"I'm not making it up," Bryan protested. "You said Duke was the victim of a botched nuclear test, then you took Dad's barbecue lighter and melted half his face off."

"Jason Myers," Diane muttered. "What have we discussed about respecting your brother's things-"

Jason looked from his mother to his father, who crossed his arms and shook his head disapprovingly at his oldest son.

"All right, maybe I was playing a little rough with his action figures…"

"So… it smelled like burning plastic?" Alex asked.

"Yeah, actually it kind of did," Ray said. "Good call, Bryan."

"Is there anything else you can think of?" Alex asked. When no one spoke up, she pulled a card from her pocket and handed it to Ray. "If you think of something, just give me a call. I appreciate the help."

Knudsen was nowhere in sight when Alex returned to the taped off perimeter. The crowd at the scene had thinned. Mike Peterson was talking with Jim Burgess as she approached the body.

"Jim," Alex called to the photographer. "Can you come over here?"

"You see something?" Burgess asked as they walked over.

"Not yet, but indulge me, just in case something jumps out at me. Peterson, would you do the honors?"

"Sure thing," Peterson said as he pulled the sheet away.

Alex crouched beside the body, resting a hand on the hot pavement as she leaned in close, studying the victim's face. The features were gone. Everything around the head, neck, and torso was burned away. The intensity of the flames had left little in their wake. As she examined the lower extremities, it appeared the fire hadn't burned with quite the same heat. She studied the hands. The right palm was burned black.

"Can you take close-ups of these, Jim?"

Burgess nodded.

Alex walked around to the passenger side door and inspected the open briefcase. As she'd noted earlier, while the interior of the case was scorched black, the exterior appeared to be unblemished. Yet, on closer examination, the leather was peppered with tiny black marks, like drippings from a grease fire that had spattered outside the pan.

She studied the details of the briefcase itself: The tanned leather body, the dark brown stitching along the seams. Brass elements glistened at the handle and on the bumpers at each corner. She studied the metal details, observing little in the way of scratches or scuffs. If she had to guess, this attaché had been newly acquired by the victim. Whether he'd bought it himself, or received it from someone else remained to be determined.

"What do you think?" Peterson asked from the driver's side door.

"Judging by his head and torso, he was looking this way when it happened," Alex began. "It appears he reflexively pulled his right hand up to protect himself."

"What are we talking about, some kind of firebomb?"

Alex nodded. "I'm guessing something in that briefcase ignited when he opened the lid." She swept her hand from the passenger seat, toward Peterson. "It happened fast, and it was moving that way. His right hand is severely burned, same as his head and neck. When he got out of the car, the flames spread down his body, but the heaviest damage was to the skin and tissue the flames struck first."

"What does that tell you?"

"That we need to figure out what kind of nasty surprise was rigged up in that briefcase."

3.

THE GUM SNAPPING PUT him over the edge.

Luke wasn't big on writing in the office during work hours anyway. While many journalists thrived on the bustling atmosphere of the newsroom, he found the background noise drove him to distraction. Curiously, restaurants and diners didn't have the same effect, probably because the people around him changed before he got to know their various idiosyncrasies and nervous ticks. His favorite places to hammer out stories were The Skyliner restaurant at the old airport, and the Five and Dime where he'd conducted the interview with Tim Givens earlier in the day.

Carley Parker, the paper's newly-installed editor-in-chief, was the only reason Luke returned to *The Daily Times* building to file his stories at all. Carley had taken over the editor's desk following the departure of Red Sanders, who had run the paper for decades, but was forced to retire in the fallout from the Gerritt scandal. As the dust settled, Puzzlebox Media, a publishing company out of Seattle, purchased *The Times* and launched the search for an experienced local editor to spearhead the paper's rehabilitation. When they learned the most qualified candidate was running a competing paper and was unwilling to jump ship, they purchased *The Aztec Review* from Carley's father – making him an offer he couldn't refuse – folded *The Review* into *The Times,* and again offered Carley the top job. This time she accepted, bringing her top reporter with her, and implementing a string of policy changes designed to boost morale and reinvigorate the paper. One of those changes included the push for reporters to spend their working hours at their desks, filing their reports in-house when they weren't out on assignment. Back in the Red Sanders days, such a request would have held little weight with Luke, but he was doing his best to honor Carley's wishes. It helped that he respected her vision for *The Times*; it never felt as though she was following some opaque, corporate agenda. Of course, the fact that they were *dating* was also a strong motivator. If Luke didn't make an appearance in the office during the workday, Carley failed to show up for dates in their off hours. Then again, as she met with a string of visiting Puzzlebox representatives to go over their paper's progress and focus on ways to boost circulation and increase *The Times'* online presence, Luke was seeing his girlfriend with less and less frequency in the evenings, whether he was sitting at his desk each day or not.

Normally, a profile like the Givens piece wrote itself. Luke would pour a cup of coffee, pop in an earbud, and transcribe the interview. Then he'd write up some introductory observations and thread in connections to past reporting and current events. The problem was his neighbor in the adjacent cubicle. Kay Griffin helmed *The Times'* advice and gossip columns, a dangerous combination if ever there was one. She was a nice enough woman, and extremely popular with readers, but her voice and personal habits got under Luke's skin. She liked to take personal calls, putting her friends on speaker phone while she worked on her nails. Kay's high-pitched guffaws, mixed with the fumes from her nail polish, gave Luke headaches. When she wasn't talking on the phone, she was scouring her mail from readers, looking for material for her columns. As she sifted through her messages, Kay would inevitably pop a piece of gum in her mouth, chewing frantically and blowing tiny bubbles as a warmup, then she'd settle into a routine. As she opened an email, she'd blow a bubble. As she read the email, she'd crack the gum in her teeth. Then she'd sigh heavily as she closed the message and filed it away. The process was the same for each piece of email and snail mail. If Kay really got into a groove, she could crack her gum more times in a five-minute period than Luke could count. Truth be told, he seldom lasted that long. The moment she snapped her first bubble, Luke would either close up his laptop and head for the Five and Dime, or grab his mug and take a break. He was in the break room, slipping the coffee pot back in the machine when Carley poked her head around the corner.

"How was the Givens interview?"

"I'm typing it up now," Luke said. "Well, trying to anyway."

"What's the problem?" Carley's eyes narrowed as she looked across the newsroom. "Kay again?"

"Yep. Have you thought anymore about my request for an office with, you know… a door?"

"I have. I just don't know how it would look. I don't want people to think I'm playing favorites."

Luke stepped forward and whispered. "But I *should* be your favorite, right?"

"Trust me, you are." She glanced over her shoulder, then leaned forward, and gave him a quick kiss. "But we're talking about work, not personal lives. I'm trying to make this a paper people *want* to write for. You remember what it was like before."

"I do, but I need a workspace where I can think straight."

"I know," Carley said as she poured herself a cup of coffee. "I'll figure something out. Just have some patience."

"I missed you this morning."

"Sorry, I had to come in early for a conference call. Some folks from the ad team are flying in today to take a look at the mid-year numbers, so I won't be back until late tonight either."

"There's always something with them, right?"

The demands on Carley's time by the new publishers were getting to be a bit much, but he didn't want to start another argument about it.

"Things will settle down eventually."

"I know," he said, hoping it was true.

"Did you ask Givens about the solar vote tonight?"

"I did. He was playing it coy, but you know his record, there's little doubt which way he'll go on that one."

"I know it's a complicated issue," Carley said. "But it would be a real shame if the city didn't come on board at this point. What Greenwood is offering is a real gift for such a small amount of funding."

"I agree. He's going to get the money either way, it makes sense for the city to jump in and have some skin in the game."

Alan Greenwood was the city's resident big idea man, a self-made billionaire, who had banked his first fortune in the old carbon energy fields, rolled those earnings into mind-blowing success with a number of early tech investments, then taken his newfound wealth and embarked on an eclectic entrepreneurial journey of his own design.

In the last decade, Greenwood had designed electric sports cars, endowed several ground-breaking departments at San Juan College, and launched any number of thriving businesses that had rattled and redefined their corresponding industries. His current obsession was solar energy, an itch he was scratching with the construction of The Greenwood Project, a sprawling solar facility in Chokecherry Canyon, not far from the epicenter of Ben

Gerritt's big hustle. The project promised to meet and *exceed* the city of Farmington's electric needs, as well as those of a handful of smaller towns in the area. Greenwood was poised to turn the local energy world on its head, and owing to the unique moral compass by which he operated, he had presented the city with an offer it would be insane to turn down; investment in the final ten percent of the facility's construction costs, with an arrangement in place ensuring the transfer of Greenwood's ownership stake over to the city, in *full*, twenty-five years after completion. Basically, Greenwood, his investors, and the people of Farmington, would split the profits according to their investment percentages for the first quarter century, after which, the city would be energy-independent from thereon out, and the original investors, save for Greenwood, would continue to share in the profits from any electricity sold outside of the city limits. Such an arrangement would mark one *hell* of a coup.

Of course, owing to the background of many on the City Council, and politics being what they were, Farmington's participation in the project wasn't a sure thing. Plenty of people around town were questioning Greenwood's motives and general sincerity, assuming he had some legal loophole woven into the final contract that would give him an out if greed got the better of him. Why would he need taxpayers to invest *anything* in the project, if he just planned to give the bulk of the place to them for *free* twenty-five years down the road? Surely, he was using the city somehow, getting them to loosen regulations while footing the bill with a sucker's bet.

Given everything they'd covered as journalists, Luke and Carley should have been every bit as cynical as the skeptics, but from what they'd seen of Alan Greenwood, they took him at his word. He came up with wild ideas and made them a reality, and in Luke's experience, that was just the sort of person who made whimsical, inexplicable decisions of the heart, and followed through on them for reasons pragmatic cynics would never understand. Of course, Luke had also reported on many a public do-gooder who turned out to be a deceptive, moneygrubbing bastard, so on principle, he watched *everyone* out of the corner of his eye, just to avoid surprises. With Greenwood he would do no different.

Whichever way the vote went tonight, it had been an interesting story to follow, one *The Times* had spilled a lot of ink covering. Whatever the final tally, there were *bound* to be more twists and turns to come.

Luke followed Carley as she walked through the newsroom to her office, passing Kay, whose phone was pressed between her shoulder and chin as she ran an Emory board over her nails.

"Frank Decca was at the Country Palace with *her*?!" Kay exclaimed as she grabbed a pen and started taking notes. "Well, I told his wife to lawyer up last year, but she wanted to give it another try. I said, 'If they've done it once, they'll do it again,' and believe me, he has done it much more than once! What's that? Oh yeah, back in '92 with one of the lunch ladies at Ladera. In '93 with the Aztec dog catcher. And in '97 with the lady who ran the Seven Two Eleven on 30th. Yeah, the one with the red beehive. How do I know? The dog catcher and the lunch lady wrote in for advice!"

"Did you hear that?!" Luke asked when they got back to Carley's office.

"Of course I did," Carley said as she took a seat at her desk. "The whole office heard it."

"I can't believe we haven't had a lawsuit over the local advice columnist and the local gossip columnist being the same person!"

"I talked to the Puzzlebox guys about it, but they say she gets readers. Actually, her column is starting to get national traffic if you can believe it."

"That's so depressing," Luke muttered. "People must think this is *Green Acres* with the way she presents things!"

The phone rang and Carley answered it.

"Yeah. Where was this? OK, we'll see what we can find out."

She hung up.

"Who was that?"

"Mike Oliver over at Station 6. He said they responded to some sort of car fire out on 170 this afternoon."

"Everyone all right?"

"One fatality. Sounds like there were some unusual circumstances. Think you could…"

"I'll stop by the station after the council meeting tonight and see what I can find out." Luke looked at his watch. "Speaking of which, if I'm going to get the Givens piece filed before tonight's vote, I'd better head over to my *other* office and get to work. Will I see you tonight?"

"Hopefully," Carley said. "But it will be another late one."

"I'll wait up."

4.

CITY HALL AND THE Farmington Police Department headquarters were located right next to each another, just down the hill from the old airport. Over the years, Luke had puzzled over the public planning that had put these facilities in such close proximity to one another – a building full of politicians, next to the jail, next to a means of quick escape – but he had yet to come up with a sound theory. Were he still alive, Mike Murphy would no doubt have recalled all the twisted bits of logic and coercion that had gone into the decision-making; he'd always known a little bit about everything he shouldn't. Fortunately, for Luke, his father's files remained at the house, where they continued to come in handy from time to time.

Luke parked between the two buildings. If he'd arrived just a little earlier, he'd have visited the crime lab before the council meeting, but it made little difference, he'd just stop in after the vote. As he was climbing out of his car, he spotted a bearded man with a camera bag crossing the parking lot. He'd dealt with Jim Burgess several times over the years when the paper was looking for an official crime scene photo to accompany a story.

"Jim, you're here late."

"Yeah, wrapping up a job for the new investigator."

"Anything I should know about?"

"Kind of a freak thing out on 170 today-"

"The car fire? You were working that?"

Burgess nodded. "It was more than just a car fire though…"

"How do you mean?" Luke asked. His story sense was going off.

"Let's just say it wasn't exactly an accident."

"Can you give some details?"

Burgess narrowed his eyes. "I'd better not. This new detective is real funny about leaks."

"Oh yeah? I haven't met her yet…"

"I like her," Burgess said as he started for his car. "I just don't want to get on her bad side."

"I understand completely."

Jason would fill him in later, no doubt.

Luke headed for City Hall, pondering the best way to approach the department's newest investigator. He had yet to meet her, partly because there had been no reason for their paths to cross, but mostly because he'd been close with the last person to have her job. Meeting Mick Gridley's successor would be a painful reminder of his old friend, and what had happened to him.

Council meetings took place the first and second Tuesdays of each month, beginning at 6 p.m. The agendas were public knowledge, with the bulk of the new business being either exhaustive recaps of *old* business, or endless debates over city initiatives and infrastructure issues. Given Farmington's long history of economic booms and busts, the matters before the council frequently swung between proactive initiatives for the future – stuff they probably *ought* to do while they had the money – and problems they needed to address *immediately* after kicking the can down the road for decades.

FIREPOWER

Tonight's solar vote was a hot button issue for any number of reasons. Depending on a person's outlook and political persuasions, they might view public investment in Greenwood's solar project as utterly foolhardy or a wise investment for the future. Yet, no matter what side of the issue people came down on, it was clearly a topic that had caught the public's attention, particularly with elections coming up, so interest in tonight's decisive vote was intense.

Of course, these being such regular events, that interest didn't exactly translate into blockbuster attendance numbers. Mercifully, Luke didn't cover *every* meeting, but he'd been to enough of them that he could pick out the regulars. In the back of the room, an agitated woman with blue hair, jiggly arms, and a tendency to shake her head dismissively at everyone who spoke, had taken up her customary spot and pulled out her knitting. That was Darla Parker. In the front row, Flap Jackson, an older man with a concave chest and a camouflage vest, was flipping through *The Economist*. Darla and Flap went to every meeting, and had been doing so for years. There were a few fresh faces in the crowd as well. A pack of Boy Scouts was seated in the second row, probably there for some sort of local government merit badge. And a group of high school kids with pro-solar signs written out on oak-tag were seated together in the center row. They appeared to be evenly divided between the leaders of the group, who were eager to stand up and make their opinions known, and the more reserved kids, who sat with their signs resting against their feet, waiting for the signal to join in the action.

A folding table with drinks and refreshments was set up at the back of the room. Luke grabbed a cup of coffee, made his way down the aisle, and waited for the meeting to get underway. The five council members filed in. Councilman Maynard and Councilman Sharpe arrived together. They were deep in discussion as they took their seats, likely debating the issue right up until the final vote. Tim Givens was next, speaking into his cell phone as he strolled in alone and sat down, continuing his conversation into the handset as he peered around the room. He was followed by a scowling, ginger-haired woman in jeans and a button up shirt, who plunked down at the front desk and began flipping through a well-worn binder of solar impact studies with over-the-top intensity; her name was Red Haubert, and unless she'd undergone some biblical change of heart, Luke had her pegged as a hard "no." Red was followed by the final member of the council, a gentleman with a neatly trimmed beard and close-cropped hair. This was Erik Kuhl, a highly successful organic farmer by day, and easily the most progressive councilman at the table. If any one member could be seen as the driving force behind the city's serious exploration of the solar project, it was Kuhl. He wasn't just a fan of solar, he was a true believer, and as a result, he'd sunk every bit of his political capital into pursuing the city's investment in the project. He was determined to push it over the finish line.

Kuhl sat at the end of the table and surveyed the room. He flashed a fleeting smile at Luke, then looked to the back, nodding solemnly as a tall man with icy blue eyes, flowing white hair, and an etched face, entered and took a seat in the last row. This was Alan Greenwood, the man who had set this whole issue in motion.

Whether the city plunked its money down or not, the project was happening, the only question was who would ultimately profit from the endeavor. Kuhl believed the city could write its own ticket if it could one day attain energy independence, while skeptics felt the project would ultimately fail to pay out, leaving the city on the hook for millions, with little or nothing to show for it in the decades to come, while simultaneously cutting its key industries off at the knees

The energy in the room shifted at the top of the hour. Givens hung up his phone as the final stragglers wandered in. Kuhl banged his gavel on the table, bringing the meeting to order.

"Ladies and gentlemen, please take your seats." Councilman Kuhl nodded to his colleagues down the length of the table as he waited for the attendees to quiet down. Once things had settled, he cleared his throat and began the meeting. "I think we've pretty well talked tonight's *primary* topic into the ground, so unless anyone has any last-minute pleas, concerns, or general threats to convey to the council, what do you say we tick a few outstanding to-do items off our list, and get to the evening's final vote? Anyone object?"

The group of students murmured amongst themselves and raised their signs uncertainly.

Someone in the back of the room coughed.

"OK, then. The first item on tonight's agenda is new pins for the Civitan Golf Course. The Park's Department-"

"Pins?!" Flap Jackson demanded from the front row.

"Yes," Kuhl answered, unfazed by the interruption.

"What kind of *pins?*"

"You know, the little flags on the putting greens."

"Jesus Christ!" Flap exclaimed.

"Indeed," Kuhl said with a nod. "At any rate, it seems the pins have faded after just two seasons, so they're hoping to replace them with higher quality-"

"The hell with the pins!" Darla shouted. "Get to the solar vote! I want to know whether or not I'm gonna have to pay an electric bill in twenty-five years."

Judging by Darla's age and overall health, Luke wondered if she'd be paying a bill in *five* years, but not for any reason she'd want to hear about.

"So anyway," Erik continued. "New pins, a show of hands?"

All five members agreed to the upgrade.

"The next item-"

"Get to the dadgummed vote!" Flap shouted again.

Kuhl seemed as eager as the rest of them to move ahead with new business. "Anyone mind if we bump Ladera's fluoride rinse program to the next meeting and proceed with the solar project vote?"

"Not at all," Givens said. "Let's bump one socialized program aside for another."

A smattering of attendees chuckled.

"Be careful or I'll take that as a vote in favor, Tim. We'll revisit the Ladera issue in two weeks and press on with tonight's primary business. Nancy, please record the votes." Kuhl said to the stenographer up front. "The issue before the council is whether the City of Farmington should contribute final construction costs to The Greenwood Solar Project as detailed in the proposal set before the council by Greenwood Renewables. Without further discussion, can I see a showing of those who are against the city taking this step..."

Two people at the table raised their hands. Red Haubert and Tim Givens. A tight smile emerged on Kuhl's face, one that quickly stretched into a broad grin as it became clear the numbers were overwhelmingly in his favor.

"And now, those in favor of making this investment in the city's future?"

Kuhl, along with the other two members at the table, raised their hands.

Luke watched Red Haubert's shoulders drop. Her face pinched in frustration as Kuhl banged his gavel triumphantly.

"The yays have it," he said. "Farmington, New Mexico is prepared to take one giant step into the energy future."

"And one enormous leap toward economic instability," Givens responded.

"We shall see," Kuhl countered happily. "We shall see."

Without uttering a word, Red Haubert got to her feet, picked up her binder, and hurled it in Alan Greenwood's direction. The throw went wild, the binder missing its target and ricocheting off the back wall, pages tearing loose and scattering across the floor as Haubert marched up the aisle and stormed out.

"Well," Kuhl deadpanned. "I take it Councilwoman Haubert will not be attending the ribbon cutting ceremony…"

The remainder of the proceedings wrapped up quickly, then the crowd was set free to clear out the snack table and guzzle the last of the low-grade coffee. Luke made a couple of notes in his reporter's pad, but there was little nuance to record in such a clear win.

"Luke Murphy?" a deep, relaxed voice asked.

"Yes?" Luke replied. He crumpled up his coffee cup and turned around to see Alan Greenwood standing behind him.

"I've been following your stories in the paper. You've somehow managed to make solar energy sound *interesting*," Greenwood said with a laugh.

"I don't know about that," Luke replied as they shook hands. "But that's nice of you to say."

"Alan, I'm looking forward to working with you on this!" Erik Kuhl exclaimed as he crossed the room.

"I was just telling Mr. Murphy here that he's managed to make solar energy sound exciting in his articles-" Greenwood said as he released his grip and patted Erik on the shoulder.

"Solar *is* exciting!" Kuhl said.

Greenwood gave Luke a knowing wink. He was passionate about the issue, but he had no illusions about the adrenaline highs, or lack thereof, that had accompanied the long public debate leading up to the decision.

Kuhl's enthusiasm left him oblivious to the fact that he'd horned in on their conversation. As the councilman plowed ahead, discussing the next steps for the project, Luke began moving quietly toward the exit. Finally, Greenwood held up his hand to silence Kuhl, and reached into his blazer pocket to pull out a business card, which he handed to Luke.

"If you ever want to take a tour of the facility for the paper, I'd be happy to have my assistant set something up," he said. "This is her direct line."

"That would be terrific," Luke replied.

"Congratulations on the vote," Councilman Givens called over as he started to leave. "I just hope you're not looking to the council for additional funding when the project comes up short."

Greenwood smiled patiently, while Kuhl rolled his eyes and continued their discussion.

Luke tucked Greenwood's card into his shirt pocket, and quietly slipped outside.

5.

THE NIGHT APPEARED TO be off to a peaceful start as Luke entered police headquarters. The uniformed officer at the front desk was leaning back in her chair, absorbed in a paperback romance. She glanced up, recognized him, and flashed a fleeting smile before returning to her book. Luke strolled past the desk and down the main corridor. He rounded a corner at the end of the hall, and ducked into the crime lab, where a bushy-haired lab worker was hunched over a metal table in the center of the room, his back to the entrance.

"Evening, Jason. You have a minute?"

"Why?" Jason Croatto murmured without turning around.

"Well, hello to you, *too.*"

"I'm sorry, you just have a way of popping up around here when I'm working on things I shouldn't be discussing with the public."

"I'm not the public. I'm the press."

"Even worse."

Luke peered over Jason's shoulder, catching a glimpse of what appeared to be a burned out briefcase.

"You wouldn't by any chance be investigating the car fire out on 170, would you?"

Jason turned to face him with crossed arms. "I was afraid that was why you were here."

"What can you tell me about it?"

"Details are hard to come by at the moment."

"But you know something," Luke prodded.

Jason Croatto was one of the few folks in the Farmington Police Department who Luke could depend upon to answer his questions candidly. He regularly provided reliable off the record information, nothing that would jeopardize an investigation of course, merely enough details to point Luke in the right direction as he followed a story. Other than Mick Gridley, their departed mutual friend, Jason was Luke's closest connection in the department. Luke hadn't been in touch with him since the arrival of Gridley's successor however, and he was finding his old friend unusually evasive at the moment.

"How many fatalities were there?" Luke asked.

"Just one." Jason replied.

"How many cars involved?"

"…One."

Luke nodded toward the briefcase. "What's that?"

"Look, Luke," Jason said as he watched him from the corner of his eye. "The new detective is handling this one, and she's really not a fan of leaks, especially not to the press."

"That's never stopped you before… She must be cute."

"That is *not* why."

"Tell me about her."

"Well yeah, she's…cute. She's also a very good detective. You'll like her."

"Assuming she'll talk to me that is. It sounds like she doesn't like reporters."

"Come on, what cop does?"

"Aren't you a cop?"

"Technically, yeah," Jason laughed. "But who says *I* like you?"

"That hurts," Luke said. He clapped a hand to his chest as he strolled idly around the lab, certain his friend was watching his every move. "Well, forgetting the fact that this new investigator doesn't like you talking to reporters, I look forward to dealing with her on some future story where she apparently won't be much help to me. Can I at least ask you a few questions off the record?"

"Man, do you ever let up?" Jason asked. "You're going to get me in trouble."

"Fine, what if we don't discuss the car fire case *specifically*, but you just tell me about that item on the table? You know, just chitchat with a curious member of the public?"

"I know what you're doing," Jason said. "Look, for starters, it wasn't technically a car fire. The vehicle itself was untouched. The driver on the other hand burned to death."

"From what?"

Jason nodded at the briefcase. "That."

"What is it, a bomb?"

"Not exactly, but something along those lines." Jason pulled on a pair of latex gloves and picked up an evidence bag, along with a small metal scraper. "They dropped it off a little while ago. It was on the passenger seat of the victim's car. Clearly something inside this case burned up fast and *hot*." He pointed to the outside edges of the attaché. "But aside from a haze of tiny scorch marks toward the front here, the damage is largely relegated to the inside of the case. This is a new one for me, but I'm thinking whatever was in this case was rigged up to launch this way," he motioned from the center of the briefcase forward. "I haven't seen Jim Burgess' photos from the scene yet, but I'd be willing to bet they'll show a trail of burn marks going from the case to the driver's seat as well." He pointed a gloved finger at two charred mechanical devices secured to the interior of the case. "See those?"

"Yeah, what are they?"

"I'm guessing they're the remnants of whatever contraption was rigged up inside. Something that was tripped when the clasps were released and the top was lifted."

"Like a sort of catapult...?"

"Basically, yeah. Plus, check out the hinges. They're still intact. That and the way the burn pattern is spread, moving from the back of the case forward, makes me think this was an incendiary weapon targeting the poor bastard who opened it."

Luke watched as Jason folded the top of the plastic evidence bag open and held it against the burned interior of the case, scraping at the pitch-black residue that coated the inside.

"You smell that?" Jason asked as he scraped black flakes into the bag.

"Burned plastic. What is that?"

"Most likely polystyrene beads."

"What do those do?"

"They ensure that once the shit inside this case is on fire, it *sticks* to whatever or whoever it hits, and stays there until it's completely burned itself out. It's the same principle behind modern napalm." Jason closed up the bag and sealed it with a printed label. "This was designed to wrap around its target like a net."

"A burning net."

"Exactly."

Jason peeled off his gloves, slipped the sample bag into a manila envelope, and motioned for Luke to follow him out of the lab and down the corridor. "The question is whether the guy out on 170 *knew* he was carrying a firebomb on the seat next to him. Did he build the thing, only to accidentally set *himself* on fire. Or did someone plant this thing in his car?"

"And how do you start to figure that out?"

They stopped outside a closed door, where Croatto slipped the envelope through a drop-off slot beneath a reinforced window.

"The first step is getting this analyzed to see what the hell it was made out of. Then maybe we can start to figure out where the components came from, and go from there."

"Assuming this new detective will eventually speak to me, can you let me know when you have something? It's been a little while since I've reported on a murder." Luke pulled a card from his back pocket and handed it to his friend. "Can you give her this?"

"Sure thing." Jason said. "But don't forget, at least for now, everything we discussed is off the record."

"Don't worry. I'll just think of it as foundational research for a potential article. Have a good night," Luke started down the hall, but stopped and turned around. "By the way, what's this new detective's name anyway?"

"Spencer," Jason said. "Alex Spencer."

6.

LUKE AWOKE IN HIS bed the next morning, one hand stretched out across the empty pillow beside him. Carley hadn't made it over after her late meeting. This was becoming an all too common occurrence. After accelerating at a healthy clip for months, their relationship had begun lurching forward in fits and starts right around the time the paper changed ownership, and he and Carley were brought on board to right the ship. He understood she was under pressure to prove herself to the new management, but he was starting to chafe at his girlfriend's willingness to put work before her personal life.

Luke climbed out of bed and trudged down the hallway to the kitchen, where he flipped on the coffee maker and rubbed his bleary eyes. The early morning sunlight was streaming in through the thin curtains, igniting the dust in the stuffy air. He really needed to replace the shades with something less tattered, but he wasn't ready to pull down his late mother's handiwork. She had put them up when he was a kid, shortly before the divorce, and Luke, like his father before him apparently, was oddly sentimental about her scattered domestic touches. He parted the curtains and peered out to the unobstructed views of Chokecherry Canyon. As he opened the windows to let in fresh air, a drooping gutter along the eaves caught his eye.

Despite his initial reluctance, Luke had been living in his old man's house for the last six months. It just made sense. The place was empty and paid for, and his apartment situation had gone from inconvenient to straight up unpleasant. Once he and Carley began dating, Luke's flirtatious neighbor went from annoyingly harmless to actively unpleasant whenever she crossed paths with Carley. After one too many hostile encounters, Luke decided it made sense to move into the old house to take advantage of the greater privacy, along with a lower cost of living and some extra space.

He poured a mug of coffee and stepped outside to size up the situation with the gutters. It looked as though he might need to replace some of the wood along the overhang, but there was only one way to find out. Luke set his mug down and headed into the garage, returning with a ladder and toolbox. A couple pokes with a screwdriver confirmed the worst, the eaves were crumbling away. Yet another unwanted task on his home repair list. He was mentally tabulating what he'd need to pick up at Farmington Lumber when his phone rang.

"Hello?"

"Luke Murphy please," a friendly female voice replied.

"This is Luke."

"Luke, this is Kim from Alan Greenwood's office. Mr. Greenwood was wondering if you'd be available to take a tour of the facility this afternoon at one o'clock."

"Facility?" Luke asked.

"Yes… the new solar project." She sounded confused. "I believe you discussed it with him last night."

"Oh, right! The solar farm. Sorry, I'm still on my first cup of coffee. My short-term recall doesn't kick in until at *least* cup three."

"Oh, don't worry about it," Kim said. "I'm the exact same way. If I don't have a cup at home, and stop for a triple-shot mocha at Cryptic Grindings on the way to the office, I'm hopeless."

"Triple-shot, eh? I take it you're an addict like me then. Maybe I should try that. The same jolt at a quarter of the sipping time."

"Oh, I don't know that it saves any time, I still drink black coffee at my desk all day as well."

"A woman after my own heart!"

"It's the only way I can keep up with Mr. Greenwood."

"He doesn't waste any time, does he?"

"No, he does not. When he sets his mind to something, he wants it done yesterday." She laughed. "It's exhausting. Speaking of which, does that sound good?"

"The Cryptic mocha? It sounds *wonderful.*"

"I mean the one o'clock tour."

"Oh, right," Luke said as his eyes fell on a black town car making its way down his street. "Yeah, that sounds perfect."

"Excellent, Mr. Greenwood will meet you there. They'll be expecting you at the front gate."

Luke watched the car as it slowed, then turned into his driveway. His eyes narrowed. A woman was driving, but that wasn't Carley's vehicle.

"Thanks, Kim. Tell Mr. Greenwood I'll see him there."

"I'll do that. It was nice talking coffee with you."

"It was. I'll tell you what I think of that mocha!"

He slipped the phone into his back pocket and waited.

Sunlight flared off the windshield as the car pulled to a stop. Luke shielded his eyes as the driver climbed out and started toward him.

"Are you Luke Murphy?" she asked.

"I am," Luke replied from atop the ladder.

She was slightly taller than Carley, with shorter, sun-streaked brown hair. Her eyes were hidden by a pair of mirrored sunglasses.

"The Luke Murphy who was asking questions at the police crime lab last night?"

Uh oh.

"Yeah?" he asked warily.

She flipped open a wallet and flashed her badge. "Detective Alex Spencer."

"Oh," Luke replied as he climbed down. "Nice to meet you detective. I left a card for you with Jason."

"I got it." She slid her sunglasses to the top of her head, revealing a pair of deep brown eyes that looked him up and down. "You mind telling me what you were pressing Mr. Croatto for?"

"I wasn't *pressing* him, I was just getting some background from him."

"Background for what?"

"Just seeing if there was a story there."

"And what did you decide?"

"When I left last night, I wasn't sure what to make of it, but you stopping by here has me thinking I might be on to something."

"Don't read too much into it," Alex replied. She brushed her fingers through her hair. "Someone comes around asking questions when I'm not there, I like to find out why."

"Couldn't you just call?"

"I like to look busy bodies in the eyes," she said, studying him so directly that Luke instinctively looked away.

"Oh," he replied, afraid he might be blushing. "Look, assuming you're doing your job, you really don't need to worry about me causing you problems."

She stared at him a moment longer.

"Honestly," he continued, hearing just a hint of desperation in his tone. "I dig around, but folks will tell you, I'm nothing if not fair."

He studied her face to see if anything he was saying was sinking in. Detective Spencer was either a very tough nut to crack, or she had a poker face for the ages. Whatever the case, she was a natural beauty, with lightly tanned skin, soft features, and subtle lines tucked under her eyes and framing her mouth. He dug that look, but he'd long ago given up on trying to describe its appeal. When he complimented Carley on the sexy folds beneath her eyes, she told him what he was describing were "wrinkles," and no matter how he protested, she wouldn't accept the fact that he *liked* what he saw. Alex had some of the same qualities, along with something a little… different. She really was cute. If he wasn't already involved, he might entertain notions of-

"You've got an interesting reputation around the department," Alex said.

"The department has an interesting reputation in its own right, if you know anything about its recent history. Which I assume you do, considering the way your position became available. I was actually good friends with your predecessor. He was one of the good guys."

Finally, Alex let him off the hook. "That's the same thing Jason Croatto told me."

"You see…" Luke cracked a smile. "That was a case where me poking around proved to be a *good* thing.""

"He made that argument as well. It sounds like Detective Gridley got caught in the middle of an unfortunate situation."

"One that had been developing for a whole lot of years," Luke said. "Things definitely got out of control near the end though."

"So I've gathered. I do I think the department is on the right track now. It's going to take some rebuilding, but the folks that are there, while clearly suspicious of newbies like myself, seem to be on the up and up. I hope so at any rate."

"I do too. And if it makes you feel any better, I grew up here, and they still look at me sideways."

"You *did* bring down the hometown hero. That's gotta take some time to process."

"I suppose you're right," Luke admitted. "How are you liking Farmington? You settling in?"

She shrugged. "I'm trying to, but I haven't had a whole lot of time off."

"You wanna come in and get some coffee?"

"Maybe another time. I need to get to the office. I just wanted to come out here and-"

"Scare the shit out of me? Mission accomplished."

Alex laughed. "Look, maybe I was jumping to conclusions. I'll tell you what, assuming it won't jeopardize my investigation, I'll keep you updated on what we're finding out. And in return, maybe you can give me some tips on avoiding the pitfalls in the department and with town government."

"I can try," Luke said with a laugh, "But I'm pretty sure I fall into more pits than anyone else around here."

"In that case, maybe I can help pull you out then." She handed him her card. "At any rate, in the future, if you have questions about this case, or anything else, why don't you just come to me directly?"

Luke studied the card. "It's a deal."

"Oh, and I did get one new piece of information before I headed over here. They traced the car in that fire yesterday to a rental place in Durango, Colorado. The dead man's name is, or rather was, Buck Florquist. I don't know a thing about him, but I'm gonna start poking around."

"Buck Florquist," Luke repeated, burning the name into his memory. "That doesn't ring any bells, but I'll dig into it as well."

"Let me know what you find out," Alex said as she climbed into her car and started the engine. "I promise to do the same."

"Deal," Luke said as he watched Alex turn her car around and head back up the driveway.

7.

LUKE PUT THE TOP down before he left the house. The sun and air felt great as he drove out to The Greenwood Project. The first half of the route was paved, but the road turned to gravel and then dirt for the last several miles. The Mustang bounced and shimmied in the deepening tire tracks as Luke glanced in the rearview mirror, seeing only empty road and a ribbon of dust snaking through the air behind him.

Eventually, he drove over a crest, and was greeted by a sea of solar panels laid out in a perfectly spaced grid stretching out to the horizon and off to either side as far as the eye could see. Blinding sunlight glinted from the reflective panels. He continued on until he reached the heavily fenced perimeter of the facility and slowed to a stop at a security booth near the front gate. Luke's eyes were drawn to the loops of razor wire clamped to the top of the fencing.

"Afternoon, sir," A uniformed guard greeted him.

"Good afternoon. My name is Luke Murphy. I'm with *The Times*-"

"Yes, Mr. Murphy. Mr. Greenwood is expecting you in the main building." The guard replied. He pressed a button and the gate slid open. "Take the first left, and continue on to the end."

"Thanks," Luke said as he pulled through the gate.

The road returned to gravel inside the fence. Solar panels swept past the Mustang on either side, their surfaces practically sizzling under the hot sun. Luke turned left at the fork, and continued until he reached a towering concrete and steel structure that dominated the property's farthest corner. Black metal staircases zig-zagged up the front of the building, leading to a series of catwalks and balconies that looked out over the property. Conduit and thick cabling snaked in from the fields of panels, weaving together before they disappeared into the buildings outside walls.

Luke spotted Greenwood's signature electric car – produced by his own company and painted British racing green – parked at ground level beside a set of massive metal doors. He parked the Mustang on the far side of the doors, allowing a comfortable ten-foot gap between his car and the other vehicle. Greenwood's sleek roadster was well-known around Farmington, Luke didn't want to be the first person to put a ding in the door.

Luke climbed out of his car, and was just wondering where he should look for his host, when he heard footsteps on the walkway overhead. He looked up to see Alan Greenwood heading down the steps toward him from the second level.

"Luke Murphy!" Greenwood said in a booming voice as he descended the stairs.

"Mr. Greenwood."

"Please," he said as he reached the bottom of the stairs and shook Luke's hand. "Just call me Alan. I'm glad you could make it on such short notice."

"Not a problem, it was either this or tackling some repairs around the house, and I just couldn't deal with home projects today."

"I hear you. I've been working with an artist to restore a collection of Matisses before I have them rehung at the house. You would not *believe* the work it's taken to ensure each petal is restored to its original vibrancy, but I keep following up on Enois' progress and letting him know when something just isn't up to snuff.

Maintaining a home is a constant battle, isn't it?" He looked at Luke expectantly.

Luke blinked, taking a moment to realize Greenwood was both serious and apparently curious to hear of his own home-keeping struggles. "I, uh, need to fix a gutter," he said quietly. "Wood rot on the eaves." When Greenwood continued to stare, Luke added nervously, "And I think a rat is living in my garden."

"Rats are terrible, Luke," Greenwood muttered gravely. "They decimated the guava trees at my Maui estate back in '98. The POG juice has never been the same since we replanted the grove." He shook his head, sadly. "I'll *never* forgive those sons of bitches."

"That's understandable," Luke murmured.

Greenwood removed a small remote control from his pocket and pressed a button. The double doors parted to reveal a black golf cart.

"I'd like to give you a tour of our little project out here in the desert," he said as he led Luke to the cart and slipped behind the wheel. "Assuming you have the time of course."

"That's why I'm here."

Minutes later, the golf cart was zipping through the rows of panels, with Greenwood at the wheel of the surprisingly fast little vehicle. He turned onto the main stretch of road that separated the sea of panels, the backend fishtailing on the gravel as Luke gripped the edge of the seat.

"I had the guys at my plant install a scaled down version of the engine from my roadster," Greenwood explained as he stomped on the accelerator. "Just to give it a little more zip."

"I'd say it worked!"

"Anything specific you'd like to know about the facility?"

"What's in the building we just left?" Luke asked.

"Computers, equipment, everything that automates the site. The project has employed hundreds of workers during construction, but once it comes online, everything will be run by around 15 full time employees working from that building."

Luke removed the notebook from his back pocket, struggling to stay in his seat as he haphazardly jotted down notes. Now that he'd experienced Greenwood's lead foot, he wished he'd brought an audio recorder with him instead.

"What can you tell me about the project itself?"

"Well, you likely know the broad details already, but just for some background, The project covers more than 5 square miles. It was funded primarily by myself and an assortment of private investors. And it utilizes 1.75 million monocrystalline silicon modules on single axis trackers-"

"Which means... what?"

"Too much insider lingo?"

"Just a bit," Luke conceded.

"I forget not everyone is a green energy dweeb. What was it Roger Ebert said, jargon is the last refuge of the scoundrel? Basically, that means we have a hell of a lot of photovoltaic panels, or PV panels, following the path of the sun and turning it into electricity to power approximately 260,000 homes."

"260,000 homes... *immediately?*"

"Yes."

"That's a lot."

"That is a lot," Greenwood agreed. "One hundred percent of Farmington's electric needs, with enough left over to power several neighboring communities in this state, as well as some in the next state over."

"How far down the road are we talking?" Luke asked.

Greenwood slammed on the brakes, sending the golf cart into a slide. "This part of the road," he said with a grin as the dust swirled around them. "We can meet that capacity the moment we come online."

"How did I not understand that?"

"No one seems to. They're all convinced I'm trying to rip the city off somehow. But that's the truth. As soon as we flip the switch, The Greenwood Project can provide all the electricity the city of Farmington will ever need, and then some. The excess power can be sold to Aztec, Bloomfield, Kirtland. You name it. We're still working out the details with our partner companies, but the future is here my friend."

"You've basically built your own goldmine."

Greenwood laughed. "It's not really my goldmine though. As of last night's vote, I own my share in partnership with the city."

"But for the time being, the bulk of the income *is* yours. You'll be the one pocketing the profits, correct?"

"You make me sound like Minnesota Fats. I expect to fold a great deal of that income right back into the project. Let's just say we're racing toward the future, and the train has stopped at the platform. I'm just glad the city decided to buy a ticket and come on board."

"I have to admit, that's the part I don't get." Luke said. "Why include Farmington for such a low buy-in, especially if you intend to *give* your share to the city some time down the road? You made them an owner, when you could have kept selling them tickets."

"Generously-subsidized tickets if you ask me."

"But you didn't do that. Assuming you can produce as much electricity as you claim, and there's not some fine print, crossed-finger legalese tucked into the agreement, this is the Horatio Alger story of public works projects. Don't your business partners have a problem with that? How do you justify it?"

"Robots!"

Luke blinked. "Excuse me?"

"I forgot to mention the robots!" Greenwood said.

"I'm not sure I follow you…"

"There!" Greenwood pointed to Luke's right. "Along the edge of that panel."

Luke looked where his host was pointing, taking note of a rectangular metal device on one of the panels. It was roughly the size and shape of a pencil box. On first glance, he'd mistaken it for a piece of the framework, but on closer examination, he could just make out a row of black wheels tucked under the edge, and could see the tiny treads rolling forward, pushing a series of spinning bristles over the dusty surface of the panel. As the device rolled forward, it left a perfectly clean surface behind.

Maybe Alan Greenwood wasn't crazy.

"Those are robots?"

"Yep. Every panel is equipped with them. They clean the surfaces at regular intervals to remove dust, grime, and… residue from birds. An elegant solution to an inelegant fact of life in the desert."

"I would never have thought of it, but that's pretty clever," Luke conceded. "But back to the business of bringing the city on board. Farmington's budget is already running pretty close to the bone, and while asking them to invest just ten percent of the upfront costs seems like a great deal on paper, that's still a hefty chunk of money, when, not to be indelicate, you could easily cover the entire cost yourself. Why go the route you've chosen?"

Greenwood's face fell slightly as the delight of the robot sighting gave way to the pragmatic explanations behind his thinking. "I know I put off an…eccentric vibe, But I'm not as out of touch with reality as you might think." He stepped on the accelerator and started the cart moving in a slow U-turn, heading back the way they had come. "Simply put, I'm looking for *buy in*. I want to give my hometown something that will make a tangible difference in the lives of its citizens, but I'm only human, I need to see some skin in the game."

"That really makes that big a difference to you?"

"*Absolutely.* I'm not asking the city to buy the land, coordinate construction, and jump through all of the logistical and regulatory hoops that this facility has required. But I *am* looking for some tangible evidence that when I eventually unwind my business interests, the folks I'm bestowing with nearly limitless energy and income, *appreciate* the power I'm placing in their hands and take it seriously enough to participate in the initial investment. I figure ten percent isn't too much to ask."

"I can see where you're coming from, but how do your business partners feel about you handing out shares of the business at such a discount?"

"It doesn't alter the value of their investments. I'm sure they'd rather I was handing everything over to *them* one day, but I can do with my portion however I see fit, so that's what I'm doing. What they're making now, they'll still be making twenty-five years from now, and they're free to do what they like with their ownership percentages as well. Business is business."

"You were pursuing the project one way or the other. Construction is nearly complete. What would you have done if the council voted no?"

"We're all mature adults," Greenwood said. "If the council had voted no, I'd have flipped the table, gathered up my toys, and gone home."

"Right, I assume you're joking, but as long as we're on the topic of business and playing well with others, what do you think people connected with the power plant and the Red Mesa Coal Mine will have to say about this, now that you're set to come online and… eat their lunch for lack of a better term. I can't imagine they'll shut their doors without a fight."

"Their days were numbered already," Greenwood replied, waving off the notion. "Change is inevitable. The whole moving shark thing, right?"

"Even in their death throes, sharks can bite. You're putting a whole lot of people out of work, including everyone working for Jeff Larson over at Larson Light & Power. Between the generating station and the Red Mesa Mine, that's a lot of workers out on the street. Some of them could try to make things difficult for you."

"First of all, Jeff Larson is a friend, but he's also a coal-loving dinosaur. The man still sees fossil fuels as the future, rather than landmarks in our rearview mirror. If you ask me, it's well past time his industry went extinct."

"Can I quote you on that?"

"I'd rather you didn't, but I guess it's too late to ask that we go off the record. The benefits are just too great. Once it comes online, the project will help us eliminate 580,000 tons of carbon dioxide annually, that's like taking 2 million cars off the road over twenty years. Those numbers are hard to argue with."

"But what about people who worry about their jobs? We're talking about an entire industry, and quite a few spin-off businesses, that count on the continued operation of the old coal-fired generating station to make a living. Those jobs will be going away, and as you said yourself, this facility is largely automated, so they won't be replaced with new ones."

"Things may get ugly," Greenwood admitted. "But they usually shake out in the end. The city will eventually share in the profits, and the people of Farmington will benefit as well. I have yet to let my investors down. This truly is a three-way partnership between myself, my investors, and the people of Farmington."

"Does that mean you'll be splitting the profits three ways, as well?" Luke asked.

Greenwood forced a smile. "Not exactly."

"Can you give me a rough idea how profits *will* be distributed? Now that the city is on board, they'll be helping you take your only competitor offline. Do you know how the finances will break down once you're the only game in town?"

The motorized cart pulled up in front of the main building.

"You'd probably do better speaking to my finance guys about that," Greenwood replied. The twinkle had vanished from his eyes. "I may be a businessman, but I'm really just a dreamer."

8.

"TELL ME HE DIDN'T say that."

"I'm afraid he did."

"I'm really just a dreamer?" Carley lowered the pages of Luke's rough draft and reached for her plastic cutlery. "That's just so… *cheesy.*"

"It did strike me as a little goofy," Luke admitted. "But it didn't bother me. He was totally sincere. Actually, he seemed almost sad about it, like it hurt to consider how his ideas clashed with reality."

She looked less than convinced. "Is he delusional?"

"You tell me. I mean, the guy's life reads like an entrepreneurial greatest hits list. If everything you touched turned to gold, you might think of yourself as a dreamer too. In his case, dreaming pays quite well."

"Must be nice," Carley said as she sank a plastic knife and fork into her plate of brisket. The knife bent precariously, cutting the meat in a wiggling line as she applied pressure. "I like this place, but I wish they'd shell out for sturdier silverware."

Luke surveyed the room. They were seated at one of the Spare Rib BBQ Company's lacquered picnic tables. A red and white checked table cloth rested beneath a sheet of tempered glass, atop which sat their plates of smoked meat. The restaurant's decor was quaint, bordering on kitschy, with pie pans and various gardening paraphernalia bolted to the cinderblock walls, but the food more than made up for the simple country trappings. Carley was having the beef brisket, while Luke was eating a pulled pork sandwich and waiting for an opening to steal a bite from her plate.

"They don't really *need* stronger utensils, the meat is so tender you could cut it with a spoon."

"True," she admitted. "But for the record, the spoons bend too."

Luke reached for his root beer. They'd had this debate before.

"Did you press him on the company structure?" Carley asked. "How do his partners feel about chopping their cash cow in two and handing the City of Farmington the larger portion?"

"Yeah, but I was mostly interested in how he thought people connected to legacy businesses like the power plant will react to his Don Quixote pursuits in the canyon."

Carley crinkled her nose.

"What?"

"The Don Quixote thing doesn't really work," she said. "Maybe if he was putting up wind turbines."

"You know what I'm getting at," Luke grumbled. "Anyway, I was pressing him on job displacement when he pulled out his dreamer line. Overall, he was pretty vague about the details."

"Funny how often that seems to be the case around here, isn't it?"

"I hate to break it to you," Luke replied. "But whenever money and local government are involved, that's the case *everywhere.*"

So, what was he like?"

"Greenwood? He's fine. Out of touch, but decent. There's clearly some cutthroat pragmatism in his approach, but I do believe his heart is in the right place. He wants to create something amazing that he can leave behind as a public legacy, but it's clearly important to him that the city shares his commitment."

"It still sounds like he's out of touch with reality."

"When you get to that level, I suppose reality is what you *say* it is," Luke mused. "He really is a big picture guy, who has no problem admitting when he doesn't know something. That's refreshing. He isn't afraid to sketch out the broad outlines and leave it to someone else to color in the details. That said, he's clearly not a fan of any sort of pushback, so I can see how he's made some enemies over the years."

"Which reminds me, Kay Griffin said Red Haubert hit Greenwood with a book last night."

"It was a binder, but she missed."

"What was that about?"

"Haubert's family has business connected with the Red Mesa Coal Mine, so the solar project isn't going to help their grocery budgets any. Technically, she probably should have recused herself, but you know how that goes."

"Yes I do. Then again, if everyone followed the rules, what would we report on?"

"Exactly." Luke speared a jalapeno with his fork and popped it in his mouth. "Long live the wild west."

"Any other eventful happenings?"

"That I didn't put in the story? The final vote passed, so things should be getting interesting around here."

"Did you happen to learn anything about that fire out on 170?"

"Jason was pretty tightlipped when I stopped by after the meeting, but I got a few details. For one thing, it wasn't so much a car fire as a *driver* fire. The running theory is that a briefcase was rigged up with some sort of boobytrap that went off while he was driving."

"*Seriously?*"

"That's the theory anyway. Jason's just wondering if the driver was transporting it somewhere and it went off en route, or if he was the intended target. But like I said, he was more tightlipped than usual."

"Why was that? He's usually a reliable source."

"The new detective is supposedly a hard ass about leakers. Although, she seemed OK to me."

"You met her?"

"I did."

"In the lab?"

"No. She came by the house this morning."

Carley's eyes narrowed. "By herself?"

"Yep."

"Why?"

"To size me up I'd imagine. Find out why I was asking Jason for details."

"You're a reporter," Carley said, sounding annoyed. "You're *supposed* to lean on people for information."

"You'll get no argument from me."

"So, what's this girl's name?"

"Spencer. Detective Alex Spencer."

"Is she our age?"

If Luke didn't know any better, he'd have sworn Carley was a little jealous.

"You know I can't really tell anyone's ages anymore," he said. "I'd guess she's in her mid to late twenties."

"Did you tell her we were friends with her predecessor?"

"I did. I think it might have eased her concerns a little. She's new to town. Came up from Albuquerque. You'll be happy to know that despite the turmoil in the department, I'm still eyed suspiciously. She's getting the same treatment, so I think she's looking for someone to commiserate with."

"Was *she* able to tell you anything?"

"Just a name. The car was rented to a guy named Buck Florquist, from Durango."

"What do you know about him?"

"Nothing else. I haven't had a chance to dig into it."

"Well, see if you can get a story together for tomorrow morning."

"Sure," Luke said.

Carley seemed agitated, which made him want to turn the tables.

"You didn't come by again last night,' he noted. "Weren't you coming over after your meeting?"

"I said I'd try, but it ran long, so I figured it was better to go back to my place, rather than wake you up."

"I was up."

The waitress came by with the bill before she could answer.

"Are you getting this one, or am I?" Luke asked.

"Gee, how chivalrous," Carley joked as she rummaged through her wallet. "Seeing as the romance is gone, and I stood you up for the good of the paper last night… what do you say *The Times* gets it?"

⌒

"You know, Greenwood wasn't interested in discussing the collateral damage to people at the mine or the generating station," Luke said to Carley as they walked back from lunch. "But how would you feel about me going out and getting some workers on the record with their thoughts."

"Some background coverage sounds great."

Grace Matthews, the *Times*' receptionist, looked up from her computer as Carley and Luke passed the front desk. "Luke, this came for you."

She held up a thick manila envelope.

"Thanks, Grace."

Luke took the mailer and flipped it over in his hands. A

Farmington Police Department seal was emblazoned across the top left corner. A stamped, warning read:

"Photos. Do NOT bend. NOT FOR PUBLICATION. ~JB."

"What's that?" Carley asked.

"I have no idea," Luke said as they marched into her office, "But it came from Jim Burgess."

He unfastened the envelope and pulled out a stack of glossy 8 x 10 photographs, which he laid out in sequence across the top of Carley's desk. The first showed a bright orange, seventies era Chevette, with the driver's side door open. A short distance away, the burned and contorted remains of the driver lay sprawled out across the pavement.

"Are these from yesterday?" Carley asked.

"I think so. Alex must have given him the go ahead to send them over."

Subsequent shots showed the body from every possible angle, with police officers and investigators circling the area, searching the scene for evidence. Those were followed by close-ups of the body: The back of the head. The outstretched hands. The gaping mouth, frozen in a silent scream. Then shots of the car: License plates. Tire marks where the vehicle had skidded off the road.

Carley pointed to a photo of a motorhome as seen from across the street, with a trading post sign in the background. "I wonder what this is."

"Must be the location of the accident." Luke guessed as he set down two images looking up and down the highway.

The next sequence showed the interior of the car itself. As expected from Jason's description, everything inside look to be largely unaffected. All of the images were taken from the open passenger side door, looking through the car toward the steering wheel. There on the seat, just to the side of the shifter, was the briefcase he'd seen in the crime lab the night before.

The exterior of the attaché looked just as it had in person. The outside leather in perfect condition. The hinges holding the top to the briefcase still appeared shiny and new, there was no sign that pressure inside had threatened to tear them free of their fittings. Then the camera peaked over the top, where the burned out inside of the case painted a very different picture. There were the burned metal pieces that Jason had pointed out.

The next shot showed Alex Spencer looking in from the driver's side door, reaching forward with one hand to bring something to Jim's attention.

"Who's that?" Carley asked.

"That's Detective Spencer." Luke replied.

"Alex?"

He nodded.

"She's pretty."

She was.

The next photos followed Alex's direction: Close-ups of the interior which, from a distance, looked perfectly normal, but on closer inspection revealed a spray pattern of tiny scorch marks and burns. They started out in a narrow band, emanating from the briefcase, and gradually fanned out, the damage burning deeper into the surface of the vinyl car seats. You could almost *see* where the driver's body had absorbed the brunt of the attack as the burning substance inside the case had engulfed him.

Luke ran his fingers over the spray pattern. "This is just what Jason was expecting to see."

Carley turned to the photo of the burned body, now covered with a sheet of plastic.

"You said this guy was down here from the Durango area?"

"Yep."

"Any idea why?"

"None. I just know his name was Buck Florquist."

"And who was that?" Carley asked.

Luke shrugged as he gathered up the photos and slipped them back in the envelope. "That's the next item on my list of things to find out."

9.

Opponents of coal power were fond of searching for the Farmington Generating Station on internet mapping sites. Satellite images of the facility looked as though black paint had been brushed across a map of the Four Corners, leaving behind a carbon streak that swept from the plant's smokestacks, across the red landscape in the direction of the prevailing winds. Luke had seen these images countless times as the debate over the plant's fate raged on, but the sight of that black scar, stretching across so many miles that it was visible from space, was still jarring as he pulled the directions up on the GPS.

Though he'd driven past the plant for years, Luke had never been inside. Driving up, it was strange how everything looked and felt *exactly* as he'd imagined, from the structures towering overhead, to the blinking red lights at the tops of the smokestacks, to the gritty haze that clung to his eyelashes as the Mustang drew closer. There was a palpable sense of déjà vu, an otherworldly feeling of unease that was amplified by the curiously underpopulated feel of the place. There wasn't a soul in sight as he drove through the open checkpoint, where the rusted rolling gate was pulled off to the side, slumped against the chain-link fencing in resignation.

He drove on through the corroding buildings and soot-encrusted catwalks that loomed overhead, scanning the alleys and passageways for activity, even as the framework of the plant itself appeared to creep in on him from every side. Once or twice, he caught a fleeting glimpse of workers in hardhats on the walkways above him, moving like automatons through the haze, but only one of them gave any indication that they had seen him: A tall, thin man in his late forties or early fifties, who stopped to watch Luke drive past and pulled off his helmet to wipe sweat from his bald head. One side of the man's face drooped, as if from palsy. The two of them made fleeting eye contact, then he was gone. Other than that, Luke was deep into the heart of the place before he encountered another sign of life.

That's when the trucks showed up.

A beat-up, black F-150 materialized behind him, its dark presence drawing little attention at first. Luke wasn't even sure *when* it appeared exactly, or where it had pulled out of, but at some point, his eyes darted up to the rearview mirror, and there it was, roaring in behind him so quickly that he stepped on the gas reflexively to get some distance. No sooner did he do that, then an orange Bronco pulled out of a side alley up head, cutting off his escape route. Luke slammed on the breaks, sending the Mustang into a slide. He checked the rearview mirror, praying the driver of the pickup wouldn't slam into him from behind.

The Mustang skidded to a stop at a forty-five-degree angle, it's front fender inches from the Bronco. The worst had been avoided. For now. The truck roared up behind him, waiting until the last possible moment to hit the brakes, and kicking up a dust cloud that hung in the air as Luke climbed out of his car to see what this was all about.

A tall guy with a narrow face and a confused expression stepped out of the truck, twisting his chin around slowly as he cracked his neck. His hands dropped to his belt, sliding forward to hug the sides of a large, silver buckle with a chunk of turquois at its center. The passenger side door opened and another guy, roughly the same height and twice as wide, climbed out and walked around the truck's front fender, where he stood beside his companion, staring at Luke with beady little eyes.

"Hey, guys," Luke said as he started toward them, pulling a card from his shirt pocket and offering it to the driver as he approached. "I think there's been some misunderstanding. Luke Murphy with *The Daily Times*."

Belt Buckle moved his head in a series of staccato jerking motions as his eyes followed the card like a worm. Just when Luke thought the guy was going to reach out and snatch it away, he lunged forward, swinging a fist into Luke's stomach and following that with a punch to the side of the head that sent him tumbling to the ground. Double Wide thundered in from behind, kicking Luke in the stomach while he was down, and staggering backward to see if he would need another boot to the solar plexus.

He didn't.

"Jesus," Luke gasped as pain radiated out through his arms and legs. He struggled to sit up. "Worst welcoming committee ever."

"You're trespassing," a woman's voice murmured behind him.

Luke pulled a hand to the side of his head, checking for blood as he rolled onto his side and watched her walk around from the Bronco's passenger side door. She was thin, in her mid-fifties, with short, curly gray hair, and a face that read like a roadmap to misery. From the deep crease in her forehead, to the lines down her face, time had carved her expression into an intense scowl. Luke recognized her from somewhere.

"The hell you doing driving through my plant?" she demanded.

"I was looking for material for a story," Luke wheezed.

"I'd say you got it."

The driver of the Bronco, a glowering hulk, with thick eyebrows that knitted together above his nose, stepped up behind her as she spoke.

"Any questions?" she asked.

"Who are you?" Luke wheezed.

"Deanna Haubert. Haubert Security."

"Any relation to Councilwoman Haubert."

Deanna spit in the dirt. "Red is my sister. Got anything else?"

"Your sister..." Luke mumbled, the hazy pieces of a mental puzzle sliding into place. "In that case, yeah, there's plenty more where that came from."

"Funny," Double Wide growled as he and his cohorts moved in on him. "We were just about to say the same thing."

Luke blinked back to consciousness, his eyes rolling unmoored in their sockets, searching for something, *anything*, that his mind could latch onto.

He settled on a field of beige flowers.

Plastic discs, stamped with a petal pattern, and fastened through the center with a stainless steel screw. A mobile home ceiling. He'd know it anywhere.

The summer after his sophomore year, he'd dated a girl whose family lived in a trailer outside town. April Strauss. Much of their brief romance played out in that trailer, when her folks were at work, and they had the place to themselves. Luke had spent a lot of hours staring up at that ceiling, studying the flowers and wondering if they'd locked the door. Punched plastic flowers were burned into his brain.

Only now, instead of lying in April's bed, he was sprawled out on a hard metal floor. And instead of April's lascivious grin, he was jolted awake by Deanna Haubert's scowling mug.

Reality was a cruel wakeup call.

He sat up with a groan, looking around the unfamiliar trailer, which appeared to be some sort of field office. A row of beat up metal desks was pushed against one wall, lined up beneath a casement window and a large map. A file cabinet sat next to the door, handheld radios, flashlights, and a coffee maker were stacked on top. Belt Buckle, Double Wide, and The Brow stood off to the side.

"You're up," Haubert observed. "Would you like some coffee?"

"Sure," Luke muttered. "I'd say hit me with your best shot…"

"But we already did." Double Wide cackled.

"Boys, come on now, Mr. Murphy here is a member of the *press*. We need to treat him like the esteemed guest that he is."

Belt Buckle looked over from the coffee station, "Sugar and cream, Mr. Murphy?"

"Black is fine." Luke's eyes narrowed. A person could get whiplash from the changes in tone around here. "Weren't you guys just kicking the shit out of me?"

"And now we're getting you coffee," Belt Buckle replied.

"Roll with the punches, Luke," Double Wide giggled.

"I apologize," Haubert said, "My employees joke, but we made a call over to your paper while you were… resting, and you check out. Sorry for the trouble, but we can never be too vigilant when it comes to protecting our contracted properties."

Luke considered suggesting a few ways they could probably be a *bit* less vigilant, but he opted to bite his tongue. Best to play along and get the hell out of there.

"Which properties are those?" he asked instead.

"Oh, you probably know already," Deanna said. "The Farmington Generating Station, the Red Mesa Mine, a few of Mr. Larson's homes. Whatever's needed, we cover it."

Jeff Larson was the head of Larson Light & Power, which had built the Farmington Generating Station decades ago, and still ran its daily operations. Luke had never met him, but the man's reputation preceded him. By all accounts, he was an OK guy who had made a fortune as the head of the company, and whose father had made a similar killing when *he* was in charge of the same business. Larson Light & Power owned the Red Mesa Mine as well. Owing to the generating station, they were also the mine's largest and *only* client.

So, this was Red's sister. No wonder the Councilwoman had been a hard 'no' when it came to Greenwood's solar project. The Haubert family business literally depended on circling the wagons around the coal industry.

Deanna flashed that wicked smile of hers. "After we talked to your paper, we made a call over to Mr. Larson's office."

Luke's head shot up.

"He said he'd be over shortly to give you a… personal tour of the plant."

"Sorry about all that," Jeff Larson said outside as he led Luke down the steps to a waiting and well-weathered golf cart. "Deanna and her boys can get a little carried away, but you can't beat their rates."

"Assuming insurance or law enforcement don't get involved, right?" Luke muttered.

He wasn't planning on stirring up trouble, but he sure as hell wasn't going to let Larson think what had happened was acceptable.

And if the Haubert folks really *had* called *The Times*, he knew Carley would be raising holy hell the moment news of the incident got back to her.

"Well, technically you *were* trespassing," Larson said as he slipped his thumbs under the straps of his suspenders.

Jeff Larson was an odd duck, an outwardly jovial fellow, with a laugh that reminded Luke of the chuckling doctor from *The Simpsons,* but he was also a notoriously by-the-book stickler, who could smile and joke even as he was putting you on notice that his lawyer was drawing up paperwork over some middling technicality. Though he was involved in quite a few organizations and clubs around town, as well as countless business enterprises, his fickle nature and nitpicking inflexibility invariably rubbed people the wrong way. And though he'd lived in Farmington for every one of his 56 years, he had no close friends and no children, just a handful of ex-wives, most of whom had left town before the ink on their divorce settlements had even dried. In short, Jeff Larson was the type of person you treated politely and carefully, but kept at a safe distance.

Though neither man would have welcomed the comparison, Luke was beginning to detect a few similarities between Jeff Larson and Alan Greenwood, ranging from their outwardly friendly first impressions – masking pricklier personalities – to their mutual tendency to brush away requests for information they didn't have or care to consider, to their shared fondness for golf cart driving tours. Fittingly, whereas Greenwood's cart was an electric model that hummed along quietly and cleanly, Larson's cart let out a series of guttural rattles before kicking out a cloud of black smoke as it accelerated.

Luke opted to drop discussion of his unwarranted assault, and make the most of their one on one time to get some information out of his tour guide.

"Exactly what kind of article are you out here to write?" Larson asked warily as he steered the cart through the plant.

"If you've read the paper for the last six months, you probably know we've been covering the whole solar proposal in depth. And I assume you're well aware of the council's vote this week, so I'm interested in covering the other side of the story, sort of the status quo for energy production and what happens next. I assure you, there's no hidden agenda. No gotcha questions or anything."

"All right. What do you want to know?"

"Just give me your go-to sale pitch for the plant? How much power do you put out? How many customers do you serve?"

"Well, we serve everybody. If you can see a home from the top of Shiprock, we produce the power that keeps its lights on."

"And how long has that been the case?"

"Since my father and his partners bought the facility in 1960 and started to expand. The plant was here before that," he chuckled at some unheard joke. "But it was a much more ramshackle operation. There were a handful of plants in the area, providing patchwork coverage for the region. Some of those closed down. Some of them we absorbed. But the generating station has been meeting the energy needs of Farmington and the region for roughly 60 years."

"And it's all coal powered?"

"One hundred percent."

"And that coal comes from where?"

"That comes from the Red Mesa Mine.

"Which Larson Light & Power also owns."

Larson nodded. "We've grown both businesses together."

"And Deanna Haubert provides security for the two properties?"

"That's right."

"How is this week's decision going to affect you all?"

Larson's hands gripped the steering wheel a little tighter as he took a breath and rounded a corner.

"Well, it's obviously not ideal, but we've seen his possibility coming for a while now, so we haven't been caught totally by surprise. We still have our fingers crossed that something will fall through, or Greenwood and his people will come up short on the service they've been promising, but if not, we have a few options on the table to spin off the business."

"Is one of those options selling the factory to Bloomfield?"

Larson nodded. "That's one…"

As talks over the solar project had heated up, the neighboring city of Bloomfield, which had bought power from the generating station for decades, had reached out to discuss purchasing the station for themselves, thereby attaining their own energy independence, albeit on a much dirtier and smaller scale than the opportunity Greenwood had offered Farmington. The Bloomfield proposal had quickly become another contentious point of debate, at least partly due to the fact that Greenwood's investors hoped to reach out to Bloomfield and other such communities and sell them *their* surplus power, again usurping Larson's business, while keeping Bloomfield dependent on an outside energy provider.

"To be honest with you," Larson said, expanding on his response. "The idea of selling my father's company makes me sick to my stomach, but it might be the only way to ensure workers at this plant and the Red Mesa Mine can stay employed."

"Any idea how Bloomfield would bankroll that kind of a purchase?"

"I assume it would involve some sort of partnership with an outside investment group, just like with the solar plant. Interest would be high, since there are a lot of target rich communities we could try to keep or take on, again, assuming Greenwood doesn't get them. But that's the kind of thing that would need to be hammered out. You'd need to talk to my business guys about that."

Another echo of Alan Greenwood.

"Who would own it, then?" Luke pressed.

Larson chuckled. "Things are always a little vague when it comes to the energy industry."

"So I'm learning," Luke replied.

"This isn't always a pretty business, Luke. I've got no illusions about that. I mean, look at this place, it's filthy, it's falling apart, but it's a necessary evil, right? You've gotta do what you've gotta do."

The cart rounded the corner and stopped at the exit to the plant. Someone, likely one of Haubert's goons, had parked Luke's Mustang beside the sagging gate. Whoever it was, Luke hoped they knew how to drive stick. The last thing he wanted was another service bill from Nick's Auto Repair.

"This you?" Larson asked as he pulled up alongside the Mustang.

"It is."

"Listen, Luke, do you like Blake's?"

"Blakes?"

"Blake's Lotaburger. You like their food?"

"Sure."

He actually *loved* Lotaburger, but the non-sequitur had him puzzled.

"Excellent," Larson says as he pulled away. "I'll have my secretary send a few gift certificates over to your office to make up for the poundin'."

10.

Luke was atop the ladder, taking measurements for the dreaded gutter repair project, when Alex pulled into his driveway.

"Weren't you up there the last time I was here?"

"Unfortunately, yes," he muttered as he climbed down. "I put it off for as long as I could, but I keep hearing my old man telling me to fix the damn thing."

"Does he live with you?" Alex asked.

She slid her sunglasses to the top of her head, and Luke once again noticed just how striking her eyes were.

"Does who live with me?"

"Your father…"

"Oh, sorry. I didn't mean I heard him literally," Luke said, realizing the confusion. "My dad passed away a couple years ago. It's just… this was his house. I guess it's not *him* I'm hearing, so much as it's my conscience telling me to fix some stuff around here."

"I can understand that. Was he handy?"

"Dad? I wouldn't say handy so much as handsy, but he taught me everything I know… about home repair."

"OK."

"I don't mean I'm handsy-"

"I get it," Alex said.

Luke tossed the tape measure aside and nonchalantly tried to put his hands in pant pockets that weren't there.

"I don't really know what to do with my hands now," he said.

Alex laughed.

"What brings you back out this way?"

"Buck Florquist."

"The guy in the car?"

She nodded. "I learned a bit more about him. Nothing that cracks the case, just a few breadcrumbs I wanted to share."

"Judging by his wheels, I'm guessing he wasn't a high-level executive in town on business."

"Captain Knudsen would take offense on behalf of the car, but yeah, he was pretty much a low-level nobody who rented a cabin on Vallecito Lake outside Durango. His employment history is spotty at best. There's no sign of a regular job for at least the last twenty years, just scattered consulting work."

"In what field?"

"According to his landlord, something to do with power plants."

The hairs on the back of Luke's neck bristled. "Like generating stations?"

"That's what I assume. The guy wasn't sure of Florquist's area of expertise, but thought he'd been involved in upgrades to Jeff Larson's facility in the late-80s, and he'd been talking to some folks in Bloomfield government recently about a few possible scenarios. Haven't you been running some stories about that lately?"

"I have," Luke said. "I was actually just talking to Jeff Larson as well."

"About what?"

"Bloomfield's utility aspirations, among other things. Any idea what Florquist was doing in town?"

"Nope. I haven't been able to find any recent Farmington connections. He had no family in the area. He wasn't married."

"Girlfriend?" Luke asked.

"Not that we know of, but we're still looking into everything. With luck, maybe we can trace some of his bank transactions and see where he might have been just before the fire. That might not go anywhere though."

"Why's that?"

"His landlord said he paid his rent each month in cash. In my experience, people who do that, tend to keep as much off the books as possible."

"What about the rental car? How did he pay for that?"

"Cash."

"*Really?* I didn't think they did that."

"The owner of the rental lot was literally named *Biff,* so... this wasn't exactly Enterprise that he was dealing with. I mean, for starters, they rented him a friggin' *Chevette.*"

"Fair enough," Luke said. "The all cash thing seems sketchy though, right?"

"What can I say? People are sketchballs, particularly the ones that pop up on my radar. One interesting development though, we were able to go over his cabin with Colorado authorities. There was nothing at his residence that could have been used to build that briefcase device."

"Really?" Luke said, pausing briefly to process what that might mean. "Well, if we're going on the assumption that whatever was in that briefcase was given to him, then we need to find out who the last person was that Buck Florquist met with in person."

"Correct."

"If the only possible connection we have to go on is the power plant, the next time I see Jeff Larson, why don't I just ask him to give me some names connected to the rumored Bloomfield power plant sale?"

"Can you do that?"

"Sure, why not? The worst he can say is no, right? Besides, he sent me some gift certificates that I need to thank him for. I'll just make sure I call ahead this time."

"Gift certificates?"

"It's a long story," Luke said, rubbing a hand on his still sore ribs. "Do you like Lotaburger?"

"I've never had it."

"You've never had *Lotaburger?* Don't they have them down in Albuquerque?"

"They do, I've just never been."

Luke stared at her in stony silence.

"What?" she asked.

"What…is…wrong with you?"

"I didn't say I'd *never* try it." Alex laughed. "I've just never thought to go there."

"Tell you what. How about I talk to Jeff Larson, and we meet in a day or two, over some burgers and shakes, and compare notes. I'm curious to hear the latest on how Farmington's boys in blue are welcoming you."

"I'm afraid not much has changed there," Alex said as she started for her car. "But sure, give me a call when you have something."

11.

ALAN GREENWOOD'S MANSION WAS the stuff of legend in Farmington, a towering stucco and timber structure, covering some 10,000 square feet, most of it comprised of cantilevered triangular overhangs, walls of etched glass, and expansive Spanish tile floors. The enormous home was set into a hillside, where it looked out over the city like an alien spacecraft that had landed in the desert to observe life in the American Southwest. As a kid, Luke and his friends used to ride out to it on their BMX dirt bikes, milling around the bottom of the driveway as they shared theories about who lived there and what their lives must be like. Greenwood had commissioned the place the moment he first hit it big, and despite his billowing success over the ensuing decades, he'd done little to update the home's outward appearance. The result was a structure dripping with the style and trappings of the era in which it was built. Luke had come to think of the place as Tony Stark's mansion, circa the *Iron Man* comics of the 1980s. Sure, it was showing its age, but as far as he was concerned, it looked just cool as ever.

"I've wanted to see the inside of this place since I was a kid," Luke murmured as he steered the Mustang through the open gates of 4202 Saint Michaels Drive and started up the long, winding driveway.

"Tonight is your lucky night," Carley said. She shielded her eyes from the light of the setting sun as they reached the top of the hillside. "It's a little tacky if you ask me. This guy is obviously a lifelong bachelor."

"I think it looks awesome," Luke enthused as he pulled under the overhang and fidgeted with his tie.

"You look great," Carley said.

"You do too," he replied as the attendant opened her door.

Luke handed the valet his keys and paused, not for the first time, to admire his girlfriend's beauty. She was *always* gorgeous, but when she dressed for a formal event, Carley was a knockout. Tonight, she was wearing a shimmering silver gown, with her hair up in a style she only wore for special occasions, in this case it was for the black-tie gala Alan Greenwood was throwing to celebrate the impending launch of the solar project. The party had been the talk of the town for weeks, and the building excitement had succeeded in drawing in the city's most notable residents and bigwigs. Whether or not they were onboard with Greenwood's renewable energy aspirations was beside the point, *everyone* was there.

Carley smoothed the front of her dress as Luke walked around to meet her. She took a deep breath and raised her chin.

"You ready for this?"

"As ready as I'll ever be," Luke said as he took her hand and led her up the front steps.

They passed through a set of intricately carved wooden doors, emerging in an airy foyer that looked out over a sprawling living room already filled to capacity. A staircase led from the entryway to the main floor below, where an expansive Dale Chihuly chandelier hung above the space like a flaming orange and red sun, its glass tendrils flaring out over the room full of partygoers. A trio of musicians played music at a tasteful volume as the guests sipped cocktails and mingled before a wall of floor to ceiling windows that offered a panoramic view of the city as a quintessential New Mexico sunset burned red over the skyline.

Luke's eyes had just settled on a heavy wooden bench near the top of the stairs that was engraved with images of Kokopelli, when he heard a booming voice behind them.

"Ah, *The Daily Times* contingent!"

They turned to see Alan Greenwood walking toward them. He was dressed in a black tuxedo with an emerald green bow tie.

"I'm so glad you could make it," Greenwood said as he stepped forward to shake Luke's hand. Any tension from their previous encounter was seemingly forgotten.

"Glad to be here," Luke said. "Do you know my girlfriend Carley Parker?"

"Only by reputation," Greenwood said. "You've done an amazing job with the paper. It's better now than it's ever been as far as I'm concerned."

"I don't know about that," Carley said. "But thank you."

"You're too modest. In anyone else's hands, I'm certain it would have folded after everything that happened last year."

"He's right," Luke said to her.

"This is quite a turnout," Carley said, doing her best to change the subject.

"Your home is incredible," Luke said. "You could sell tickets."

Greenwood laughed. "No ticket required. Please, feel free to wander around and check out any parts of the house that you'd like."

"I just might do that!"

"Just be sure you make the rounds too. There are a lot of interesting people here," Greenwood said as he started down the steps to join the crowd. "Get a drink at the bar and make yourself at home."

"What do you say?" Luke asked as he took Carley's hand. "Shall we get a drink?"

"Absolutely."

They started down the stairs, scanning the crowd for familiar faces. A few guests nodded to them, people they'd crossed paths with in the course of their reporting.

"I see all but one of our city council members made it," Carley observed.

"Who's missing?"

"I haven't spotted Red Haubert yet."

"Mother's milk?" a happy voice called from the bar.

Luke looked over to see Rene, his favorite bartender from The Skyliner – the restaurant and bar at the old airport – standing behind the counter, waiting for them to approach. Rene was in his early fifties, a jovial man, with a constant twinkle in his eye. At some point, he'd taken to gently mocking Luke's signature cocktail by referring to it as mother's milk. Luke still didn't get the joke, but frankly, he didn't care. Rene, made an exceptional white Russian; they had a subtle butterscotch aftertaste, the source of which Luke struggled to pin down. He'd finally decided it was something in the cream.

"That sounds great," Luke replied.

"What about you, Carley?" Rene asked. "The usual?"

"Sure. Thanks, Rene."

"A martini for the lady, and one mother's milk for the... gentleman."

"What are you doing here, Rene?" Luke asked.

"I follow the money my friend. When Alan Greenwood is looking for wait staff, anyone who knows anything in this town drops *everything* and takes the work."

"He pays well?"

"Ohhhhh yeah."

"That's good to hear," Carley noted. "Anyone interesting here tonight?"

"Just about everyone so far as I can tell," Rene observed as he started on their drinks. "A few business bigwigs. All they ever order is that nasty imported beer in the green bottles. Senator Esmond was here earlier, walked me through some concoction called a *Beerita.*"

"What the hell is that?" Luke asked.

A Haunted look passed over Rene's face. "You don't want to know."

"Any other politicians?" Carley asked.

"Well, I've served most of the council members, some more than others if you know what I mean. Tim Givens, Councilmen Sharpe and Maynard, Erik Kuhl, the bulk of that crowd is milling around. Oh, and the mayor is right over there."

Rene nodded towards a tall man with a white flat top and a nose covered with burst capillaries. Mayor Joe Sullivan. When Ben Gerritt went down, the fallout had engulfed not just the police department, but half the city council and a wide swath of town hall, including the mayor at the time, a fellow named Happy Flanagan, who, frankly, wasn't so happy after a number of wire transfers from Ben Gerritt's associates were traced to his reelection campaign as the investigation unfolded. When the next election was over and done with, the people had voted in the tough talking, hard drinking Joe Sullivan to take Flanagan's place. A law and order candidate and former Marine, Sullivan was enjoying great popularity, due in no small part to his penchant for buying a round for the house whenever he and his wife were spotted at the Country Palace.

"What's the mayor drinking," Luke asked as Rene slid their drinks to them.

"Jack Daniels."

On the rocks?" Carley asked.

"In a glass."

"What do we owe you?" Luke asked.

"It's covered."

Luke slid him a five for a tip. "Thanks, Rene. We may be back."

"I'll put the cow on notice."

Luke shot Carley a miffed look as they collected their drinks.

"You know, I tell myself his wisecracks are in good humor," Luke murmured as they crossed the room. "But sometimes I'm not so sure."

"Rene loves you." Carley reassured him. "He just likes to throw you off balance. You're cute when you're befuddled."

"Oh."

He wasn't quite sure what to think about that either.

"This is your chance, Luke. Shall we take the self-guided tour?"

"I'm ready if you are."

The music drifted after them as Luke and Carley slipped away down a long side corridor lined with blue glass walls that were illuminated from behind to highlight air bubbles trapped in the thick, translucent plates. As expected, the house was cavernous, eclectic, and delightfully over the top. Every hallway and door seemed to open onto two more, each branching out into another wing filled with new and unexpected surprises. All together they counted six bedrooms, at least as many bathrooms, a workout room, an indoor half-court, an indoor pool and jacuzzi, an enormous kitchen (bustling with catering staff for the party), a wine cellar, a recreation room with three pool tables and dozens of classic arcade games, a bowling alley (the pins and balls glowing under purple blacklights), and last but not least, a home theater with the biggest screen Luke had seen in Farmington outside of the Cameo Theater downtown.

"How big would you say this place is?" Carley wondered as she looked down on the driveway and tennis courts from the deck that wrapped around the perimeter of the mansion.

"I've heard 10,000 square feet, but to me it feels bigger."

She turned and looked him in the eyes. "It's kind of crazy, isn't it?"

"Maybe, but I'd take it."

"You don't need all this to be happy though, right?"

She stepped forward and gave Luke a long, gentle kiss.

Luke smile and kissed her back. "More of that would be a good start. And perhaps another white Russian."

Carley flashed him a bemused look. "I'd give you a hard time, but my glass is dry too."

They made their way back through the house, re-emerging in the thick of the party. Carley headed to the bar to refill their drinks, while Luke stood and watched the crowd. As usual, the room was filled with familiar faces. Just *where* Luke knew them from, he couldn't always recall. Along with the usual assortment of men in cowboy hats and women in southwest dresses and turquoise jewelry, there were a few standout characters scattered around the room, most notably a bottle blond in her late-40s, who stood a short distance away, surrounded by a group of star struck businessmen, and sipping a Martini as she sized each of the them up. She was attractive in an excessively made up kind of way. She wasn't the kind of woman Luke would ever want to get involved with, but the sort that catches a guy's eye for a moment and sets his mind spinning. He knew her type: nothing but trouble.

"Luke Murphy, the man himself," Joe Sullivan said as he emerged from the cocktail line, a fresh drink in his hand.

"Mister Mayor," Luke said.

"I've been enjoying your coverage of this whole solar project adventure."

"Thank you." Luke said. "It's been a long and winding road, hasn't it?"

"And it's not over yet. Lots of stuff left to decide, assuming Greenwood's little experiment does what he hopes."

"You sound like a skeptic," Luke noted.

"Me? No! I'm a realist. Someone promises me electrical mana from heaven, I wait to see if it holds a charge. Besides, I'm here aren't I? What does that tell you?"

"That there's an open bar?" Luke joked.

Sullivan gave him a slow sideways look, then burst out laughing. "I like you Luke, you say it like it is, keeps us honest. But just for the record, I'm here because I believe in this thing. No skepticism here."

Luke motioned across the room. "Then just out of curiosity, why do you suppose Tim Givens is here tonight? He's about as skeptical as they come."

"Speaking as a politician, and *off the record,* he's hedging his bets. No question. To paraphrase an old song, they may be wrong, but they may be right, and if they're right, we want to be able to say we knew them when."

"So they'll open up their checkbooks and fill your coffers."

"Exactly," Sullivan said with a wink as he tossed back his Jack Daniels. "You know, you've got some backbone, Luke. I see you with your little milk drinks from time to time, but you're a hell of a lot tougher than you look. It's no wonder you took down Ben Gerritt."

The group standing next to them grew instantly quiet.

Luke cleared his throat uncomfortably. "I don't know that I 'took him down' exactly. I just stuck to the story."

"Like a coyote on a damned cat. You were out for blood the way I saw it."

Luke glanced to his side and noticed the blond with the martini pushing through the crowd toward him. Before he could speak or flinch even, she stepped forward, and in one smooth motion, flung the contents of her martini glass directly in Luke's face.

Carley returned with their drinks as the vodka was still dripping from Luke's nose. The blonde spun on her heel to leave, but stopped short as they nearly collided.

"It's OK," Carley said as she handed the woman her own fresh martini. "He tends to have that effect on women."

Luke's assailant stared Carley down for a moment before she silently accepted the drink and stormed back to her group.

"Who the heck was that?" Luke asked.

"I believe that was Melanie Gerritt," Mayor Sullivan said.

"Ben Gerritt's daughter? I thought she'd left town years ago."

"Apparently she's back," Carley said as she took Luke's white Russian for herself.

"I hope I didn't cause any trouble here," The mayor said in a way that suggested he really wasn't that concerned either way. He examined his empty glass, arching his neck to look for Rene. "Ms. Parker, good to see you again as always. Luke, I'm sure I'll be talking to you soon as well."

"Have a good night, Mayor," Luke said as he dried his face with his tie. "I really didn't do anything wrong," he whispered once they were alone.

"For once, I believe you." Carley said. Then she downed the rest of Luke's white Russian and wiped her lips. "What do you say we head to your place and I get you out of these wet clothes?"

"That sounds like just the ticket."

"You still smell like martini," Carley murmured.

She rested her head on Luke's chest as they lay together in the candlelit darkness of his bedroom.

"I thought you liked vodka."

"I do. It just makes me want more."

"More what?" he asked suggestively.

"I was thinking of more to drink, but if there's something else on your mind, I might be persuadable. Don't go thinking you're irresistible though."

"Believe me, I have no illusions when it comes to the effect I have on women. Tonight was a good reminder. This has been nice though. It had been too long."

"I know," Carley said as she watched the candle's flame flicker in the breeze from the window. "Things should be getting back to normal soon. I hope so anyway."

"Me too. It seems like there's always something unexpected coming up. Some new deadline."

"At the risk of undermining my editorial authority," Carley said as she arched her neck to look up at him. "The *hell* with deadlines."

12.

Luke woke with a glaze of sweat across his forehead. He opened his eyes to see sunlight filtering in through the bedroom curtains. Even with the windows open, the house was heating up quick. It looked like they were in for another scorcher.

He reached his arm across the bed, and was pleasantly surprised to find Carley still lying beside him. She looked up, only half-awake, and gave him a sleepy smile, one which vanished in a flash of irritation when the phone on the bedside table behind her began to ring.

She rolled over and answered it.

"Hello?" Carley said into the handset. "Just a minute."

She handed Luke the phone and watched him curiously. It had been a woman's voice on the other end.

"Yeah?" Luke asked. "Hang on, let me get the address."

He leaned out of bed and pulled a notebook and pen from the pocket of the pants he'd thrown on the floor the night before.

"Where is that exactly?" He asked as he jotted down notes. "OK. I'll be out there as soon as I can."

He hung up the phone and got out of bed.

"Who was that?" Carley asked as she watched him get dressed.

"Alex Spencer," Luke replied, picking up on the edge in her voice. "The detective I was telling you about."

"The one who keeps showing up out here. I remember."

"She's been here twice, and yes, that's the one." He pulled on a T-shirt and gave her a funny look. "Am I detecting a little jealousy?"

"It's just a little odd. Since when does the Farmington police department provide wakeup service? And isn't this the woman you said hated leaks?"

"That was before she'd met me. We've been comparing notes as we go along. Remember Buck Florquist?"

"I guess so," Carley answered, though she still looked irritated. "Where are you going?"

Luke showed her the address he'd written down.

"Alex said to go here if I wanted to break a major story."

"*Alex* huh?"

"Sorry, I meant Detective Spencer." He leaned down and kissed her, then headed for the door. "I love that you're jealous, but trust me, you have nothing to worry about."

The sun was beating down hard by the time Luke reached the scene. He parked the Mustang beside a handful of police and fire trucks lined up along the edge of the bluffs. Heatwaves were rippling from the hoods of the vehicles. Luke stepped out into the stifling air and immediately heard a voice calling to him.

"Luke, you made it!"

He turned to see Jason Croatto walking over from one of the support trucks. A satchel of supplies was slung over his shoulder. Sweat was dripping from his bushy hair.

"Jason, I'm not used to seeing you out in the field."

"I'm usually able to avoid it." Jason said as he mopped the perspiration from his brow. "I'm not made for this kind of heat, but Alex wanted me here for this one."

"What are we here for anyway?"

"Follow me."

Jason led Luke through the brush to a trailhead, where a uniformed officer was standing watch. He let them pass when Jason showed his credentials. They descended into a sandstone crevice, moving carefully to ensure their footing on the loose stone. Eventually, the space opened up, giving them a wider view of the canyon below. Luke gasped as he caught a glimpse of the main attraction.

Jason swept his arm across the landscape, following the debris field that stretched across the canyon floor. "*That* is why we're here."

"Jesus," Luke muttered as he took in the wreckage. "What happened?"

"That's what we need to figure out."

The crowd of police and fire personnel grew thicker as they reached the canyon floor.

"Was this a plane crash?" Luke asked.

"Yep. We think it was a Beechcraft Musketeer," Jason said as he led the way into the crowd of investigators and personnel who were scouring the scene for evidence. "It's a popular but older civilian aircraft."

"How long ago did it crash?" Luke asked.

"Sometime last night," Alex Spencer said from behind them.

"You weren't kidding about this being a scoop," Luke replied.

He turned around to see Alex Spencer standing alongside Jim Burgess, who was once more photographing the scene.

"Good to see you again, Luke," Burgess noted.

"Thanks for sending those photos, Jim."

"The hell is press doing here?" Captain Knudsen grumbled as he approached the group.

"He's with me," Alex noted.

"Is he now?" Knudsen muttered, eyeing Luke suspiciously. "I'd be careful of that one if I were you."

Alex waited til Knudsen had stormed away before she returned to the discussion at hand.

"I didn't realize you and Jim knew each other," she said to Luke.

"We've crossed paths a few times on stories."

"Most folks in Farmington go way back," Burgess noted.

"I'm starting to realize that now."

"Can you walk me through what happened?" Luke asked.

Alex nodded. "Just hang on one second."

She paused to give Jason instructions about what areas of the scene she was especially interested in, then she watched as he and Jim continued tagging and photographing the site. When they were a short distance away, she returned to where Luke was standing and led him to the center of the crash.

"Like I said. We think this occurred last night. We're far enough from town that no one heard it or reported any disturbance at the time, but a pilot landing at the airport this morning flew over the wreckage on his approach and called it in." She swept her arm across the scene as she spoke. "The plane went down over there, skittered across the canyon floor for a while, throwing off pieces and tearing itself apart, until it hit that outcropping," she pointed to a section of stone jutting up from the ground. "That's where it came to a complete stop, and the pilot's body was thrown clear of the plane til it smashed into the cliffs over there." She pointed to a spot some distance away, where investigators were huddled around a body covered with a plastic sheet. "The impact broke every bone in the body." She slid her sunglasses to her forehead. "As best we can tell, the pilot was dead before he went through the windshield. Before the crash even."

"How do you know that?" Luke asked.

"Notice anything interesting about the wreckage?"

Luke studied the sections of twisted and torn metal. Aside from the chipped and scraped white paint, the debris was mostly covered in red clay and dirt.

"None of it looks burned?"

"Exactly." Alex said.

They continued on, following a trail of little orange evidence flags, fluttering in the scorching hot air. As they approached the rock outcropping, and with it, the wingless hull of the plane, she bent down and pointed toward the interior of the wrecked aircraft. Just as with Buck Florquist's car, the interior of the plane, aside from being completely torn apart, was largely free of fire damage. The pilot's seat however was scorched and burned.

Alex pointed to something on the floor of the cabin.

"That look familiar to you?"

Luke's eyes settled on a briefcase with a familiar tan exterior, dark brown stitching, and brass corner pieces.

"Either Samsonite needs to issue a serious recall," Alex said. "Or someone is handing out briefcase bombs."

Luke's eyes darted over to the bluffs, where the team from the medical examiner's office was lifting the bagged body onto a stretcher to carry it up the embankment.

"Do we know who was flying this plane?" Luke asked.

"*That's* where things get interesting," Alex replied.

"Who was it?"

"The pilot was Jeff Larson."

13.

JASON HAD SET THE lab up for maximum efficiency, with Jim Burgess' photos pulled up on a large monitor to the side of a wall-mounted dry erase board. The briefcase from the scene of the plane crash was laid out on a metal table beside the identical case from the Florquist investigation. Luke leaned against the table as he waited for things to get started. It had been a long day. How Jason was still running around pulling things together was a mystery.

Alex marched into the lab and set a drink carrier down on the table. "I don't know which is the latte and which is the mocha," she said as she grabbed her own drink. "But the black coffee is mine."

Luke noticed the skull and bones logo on the sides of the cups: *Cryptic Grindings*. If he spoke to Kim in Greenwood's office again, he could tell her he'd sampled her favorite coffee.

Alex walked over to the monitor and leaned in close, examining a shot of the crash scene. She held her finger in the air just above the display, tracing the path of the plane from the area where it first struck the ground, to the rocky outcropping where it stopped short, hurtling Jeff Larson's charred remains through the windshield and into the cliffs. Debris was strewn across the site.

Luke again noted the aircraft's lack of fire damage.

"Was Larson nearly out of fuel when he crashed?"

"Yep, tanks were almost dry," Jason replied.

"Do we know if he was coming or going?"

"Judging from the approach, we think he was returning to the airport."

"Where he was coming *from* is the mystery," Alex said.

"Don't they file flight plans at the airport?" Luke asked.

"Things have gotten fairly lax up there since Mesa Airlines stopped their regular service in and out of town," Jason noted. "It's mostly just civilian pilots and business travelers these days."

"From what I gather, Jeff Larson had been flying out of there for decades. The tower controller I spoke to told me they waved him out sometime yesterday, but nobody caught the time, they didn't even know he was leaving til they saw his plane taxiing out to the runway."

Luke shook his head. "That would have been helpful information to have."

"You're telling me," Alex said. "So, what do we know? He was an experienced pilot, so we can assume he knew how much fuel was left and was coming back into town as planned before he ran out. But something happened before then, and the plane went down. No fuel. No explosion. But Jeff Larson is burned to a crisp. What do we suppose happened?"

Jason pointed to the matching briefcases on the table. "Same thing that happened to Buck Florquist out on 170, right? The case on the seat beside him was boobytrapped."

"That's what it looks like," Alex said. "Which brings us to the same question we had with Florquist. Did someone give him the case, or was he transporting it somewhere?"

"Actually, it answers one of our questions," Luke observed. "Now we know Florquist *didn't* know the case in his car was rigged. Not unless his ghost is going around handing out fire-bomb briefcases."

"That's assuming the two briefcases are the same." Alex said, turning to Jason. "They're a match," he confirmed. "Same brand. Same burn patterns and components. Same everything."

"Any fingerprints?" she asked as a hopeful afterthought.

"Only those of the victims. Florquist's are on the last briefcase. Larson's are on this one."

"I'd be inclined to believe Larson didn't know what he was carrying." Luke said. "What if we assume Florquist didn't have a clue either?"

"It's usually best to avoid assumptions," Alex said. "But just to theorize, let's go with that for now."

Luke walked over to the dry erase board, picked up a marker, and wrote out each victim's name.

"We have two men we know collaborated on a project at the generating station sometime in the past. Both were killed in a similar fashion within days of one another. I'd be willing to bet the two events are somehow related-"

"Can I interrupt here for a second?" Alex said. "This might be crossing into an ethical grey area, but just to be sure you understand, none of this can go into your reporting. Not yet anyway."

"Of course not, you don't need to worry about that," Luke reassured her before continuing on. "Just looking at people related to the power plant, who does that give us to consider?"

"Anyone who works there?" Alex said. "I mean, we have no idea what the motive could be. Disgruntled co-workers, jilted lovers, jealous husbands. It could be anyone these two guys ever crossed paths with."

"That's true, but we're also at a pivot point for the industry, it would be a hell of a coincidence if this was a personal vendetta rather than something tied into the business. Who does that give us to look at?"

"You tell me," Alex said. "You've probably met most of them. I'm still the newbie around here, remember?"

Luke thought for a moment, then started writing down names.

"Off the top of my head, there's Deanna Haubert, who supplies all of the security for the Farmington Generating Station and the Red Mesa Mine." He wrote Haubert's name on the left-hand side of the board and crossed his arms in thought. His sore ribs reminded him of the thugs who'd wailed on him when he showed up unannounced. "There's Haubert's 'security' team," he said, as he drew a stick figure caveman and 'X 3' beside it."

"Any names for those cavemen?" Alex asked.

"I don't know their Christian names, but I call them Belt Buckle, Double Wide, and The Brow."

She laughed. "OK, Deanna Haubert and her cavemen, anyone else?"

"That's it," Luke noted. "If we could figure out the last places Florquist and Larson were seen, that might give us some more suspects."

"What about the briefcases?" Alex asked. "Do they have any serial numbers or identifying mark?"

Jason shook his head. "None that I can find."

They sipped their coffees in silence as Alex flipped through the rest of the images from the crash site.

"What about Alan Greenwood?" Jason asked.

"Greenwood?" Luke was taken by surprise. "I don't know why the hell he'd be going around killing people? Besides, he was throwing a party last night, he's accounted for."

"I'm just spit balling," Jason said. "But you're making a mistake if you think he has an alibi. Not with these briefcases. They're a plant it and forget it option. Unless there's a timer, my guess is that they go off when someone pops the lid to look inside. There's nothing that says Greenwood or Haubert or whoever couldn't have planted the cases, or handed them over minutes, hours, or days before they were actually triggered…"

"That's true," Alex said. "I'm not saying Greenwood is a suspect, but there's no sense ruling anybody out. The higher up people are on the food chain, the more likely they are to engage someone else to do their dirty work. This could be a murder for hire situation too, which means the person setting things into motion can socialize in public for a nice little photo op, while someone on their payroll is out there cutting throats so to speak. We need to look at things objectively, see who stands to gain from having the two of these men out of the picture."

Luke was surprised at how defensive he felt at even the casual suggestion of Alan Greenwood's involvement, but once the idea had been planted, he had a hard time getting it out of his head. The industry *was* at a transition point, and it might actually be in Greenwood's interest if there were to be some sudden upheaval at the plant.

"Any idea if Greenwood and Florquist had anything in common?" Luke asked.

"Not as far as we know right now," Alex said. "But that could change."

Luke hesitated, then wrote Greenwood's name on the board beneath the three cavemen. He set the marker down and turned to his cohorts.

"I'd better write up the report on Jeff Larson's accident – just-the-facts, don't worry. While I'm at it, I'll see if I can follow Larson's career back and see where it might intersect with Florquist and Greenwood. Maybe there will be some overlap, but it still seems like a wild card if you ask me."

14.

LUKE SAT IN A booth at the Five and Dime, eating a Frito pie as he glanced over the Larson piece. By now, his report on the plane crash no longer counted as a scoop, but he had bigger things on his mind. He figured the piece was probably as good as it would ever get, but a voice was nagging at the back of his mind, prodding him to cast a slightly wider net before he sent the story to layout. He didn't want to stir up needless trouble, but his gut was telling him to make a call, perhaps he could get an extra quote that might shed some light on what was going on.

The hell with it.

He picked up his phone and dialed Greenwood's office.

"Good evening, Greenwood Renewables," the familiar voice answered.

"Hi, Kim. This is Luke Murphy from *The Times* calling."

"Hey! How can I help you?"

"I know this is sort of last minute, but I'm wondering if he has time to talk tonight."

"Let me check. Can I ask what this is regarding?"

"I'm hoping for some background quotes on Jeff Larson…"

There was a long pause.

"Are you still there?" Luke asked.

"I'm here. Can I put you on hold for a second?"

"Sure."

The call went quiet and Luke took the opportunity to finish the last of his Frito Pie, quickly crunching on the corn chips until Kim came back on the line.

"Luke?"

"I'm here."

"Mr. Greenwood is at home for the rest of the day, but he said you can come by the house in an hour if that works for you."

"That would be perfect. Thanks, Kim."

He hung up and called Alex.

"I don't know if this is the best move, but I'm going over to Greenwood's house to ask him about Jeff Larson."

He heard her inhale.

"What are you hoping to get out of that interview?" Alex asked.

"I don't know exactly. I just need to see the expression on his face when he talks about him."

"Don't go making him think you're-" she stopped, but he'd heard the wariness in her voice. "Please don't push things too far with this."

"Trust me, this is what I do. He told me himself they'd had past business together. At worst I get a good quote. At best… I get something juicier that will help us *both* out."

"I suppose it's worth a shot. But… be careful, Luke."

The gates were open at the bottom of the driveway when Luke arrived. The Mustang rumbled as he gave it extra gas and started up the incline. In his mind, the car was a classic, but he had no illusions when it came to the amount of mileage and wear and tear he'd put on it over the years. It wasn't all that long ago that the poor thing had taken a swim in the Animas River. The fact that it was still on the road at all was a minor miracle, it was certainly understandable that it would rattle and wheeze as it snaked up the hillside to Greenwood's estate.

A ribbon of red burned at the horizon of the black sky as Luke reached the summit and circled the drive. He pulled under the overhang, narrowly missing Greenwood's car parked in the darkness. His shoes scraped in the gravel as he felt his way around the back of the vehicle, turning his attention to the uncharacteristically dark house. Just one night earlier, the place had been lit up like a luminaria, light beaming from every window and doorway. Now, it was snuffed out like a candle.

He climbed the stairs to the entrance, fumbling for the doorbell until he set his hand on the handle and realized it was unlatched. He took a deep breath, pressed his fingers against the wood, and pushed. The door creaked open, revealing the red and orange Chihuly chandelier as it glowed dimly over the otherwise pitch black interior.

"Hello?"

Luke's voice echoed in the quiet.

He stood in the doorway, waiting for his eyes to adjust. Then he started forward, proceeding cautiously into the foyer as he did his best to recall the layout of a house he'd visited only once before. His feet slid over the Spanish tile floor as he peered to the left, looking down the length of the glass-walled corridor that led to the rest of the home. The blue light filtering through the wall panels gave the passageway an ethereal glow as it faded to black at the far end.

"Mr. Greenwood?" Luke called down the hall.

A muffled gasp came from behind him.

Luke spun around. The sound had come from the living room. He found the railing and started down the stairs, plunging deeper into the darkness as he did so. He reached the bottom and was just about to call again, when he tripped over something sprawled out across the floor. Luke dropped to knees, feeling around until his hands brushed against a leg.

He'd tripped over a body.

A jolt of panic fired through Luke's system as he leaned closer, his eyes struggling to sift details from the murky orange light. Slowly, a picture began to pull into focus. The long, flowing white hair. The etched lines of the face.

Greenwood.

He was still warm.

Luke felt for a pulse. It was there, but weak.

"Alan!" he shouted as he ran his hands over the body, trying to determine what had happened. His fingers felt something warm and slick as they passed over Greenwood's chest.

Blood.

"Alan, what happened?"

Greenwood struggled to breath, finally murmuring, almost in a sigh, "Intruder…"

"Have you been shot?" Luke whispered.

But there was no answer.

Someone had broken in. Were they still there?

Luke pulled out his phone and punched in 9-1-1, doing his best to cover the glow coming from the phone's display.

"9-1-1, what is your emergency?"

"Yes, I'm at the home of Alan Greenwood-" he whispered

"Sir, please speak up. What is your location?"

"4202 Saint Michaels Drive. I believe the owner has been shot. I need an ambulance and police assistance."

The sound of computer keys clattered in the background as the dispatcher sent out the order. *"Is the shooter still in the building?"*

"I'm not sure-"

Luke's head shot up at the sound of footsteps on the landing above.

Bam!

A shot rang out, shattering one of the Chihuly's flailing tendrils and showering the room with glass shards.

Bam!

Another shot, followed by the twang of a cable snapping above them. In the flash from the muzzle, Luke caught a glimpse of a barrel-chested man in a ski mask, standing at the top of the stairs with a pistol in his hand.

The chandelier gave way. Luke watched it plunge toward the floor, glowing dimly the entire way down, until it ran out of cable, and the weight of the glass ripped the wires from the ceiling, snuffing out the light as shattering sounds reverberated in the darkness. He shielded his eyes from the spray of splintered glass.

The room went silent.

Luke looked up, toward the pale blue glow of the corridor.

Had the gunman fled?

He listened intently as he once more attempted to recall his surroundings. The stairs to the entryway, where he'd just seen the masked figure, were straight ahead. If memory served him, the wall to his left was floor to ceiling sandstone, with a wide fireplace at its center. A wall of glass swept around the remainder of the open space, eventually meeting up with the stairs at the far end. The rest of the room was a mystery. He had no idea how it was furnished or what might be blocking his way.

Luke leaned down, placing his ear next to Alan Greenwood's mouth, listening for breathing. Just when he detected the faintest inhalation, there was a creak at the far end of the room. Luke focused his eyes on the wall of windows. He could just make out the lights of Farmington in the distance when the gunman's silhouette passed in the foreground. He was moving slowly, feeling his way through the darkness, the outline of a gun visible in his hand. His head appeared to lurch up and down as he moved, as if from a limp.

Luke held his breath, every muscle and nerve tensed and ready. He was wound up so tight that he nearly screamed when a hand seized his leg without warning.

"*Run,*" Greenwood hissed.

The muzzle of the gun swept toward them as Luke took off running at full sprint.

Bam!

Sandstone shrapnel skittered around the room as Luke pumped his arms and legs, racing for the stairs. His shin smashed into the glass edge of an unseen coffee table, and he went airborne, hurtling head over feet as his vision flashed with lightning bolts of pain. Luke twisted in the air and slammed down on his shoulder, sliding across the floor for a half dozen feet before he regained his footing and lurched forward uncertainly, clawing for the stairs.

He could hear the guy behind him, trying to catch up. Luke found the stair rail, and had just begun to climb, when he heard his pursuer tumble over an obstacle behind him.

"Dammit!" the man shouted in pain as he hit the ground.

Luke reached the top of the stairs, suddenly remembering the Kokopelli bench he'd noticed the previous night. He reached for the heavy piece of furniture, wrapped his fingers around the top, and with some effort, managed to swing it around, hurtling it down the stairs just as the gunman reached the first step.

The man grunted as he caught his foot on the bench and tumbled headfirst onto the stairs. Luke was already running down the corridor at full sprint as he heard him hit the stairs with his face, the thunk of broken bones, the tinkling of teeth. If he didn't have a limp before, he sure as hell did now.

"You're a dead man!" The man roared as Luke barreled down the corridor and dived into the black.

Damn, that was a good milkshake. Vanilla didn't get its due.

Alex set the drink on the roof of her car and fished the cheeseburger from her bag. All of Luke's Lotaburger talk had made her curious enough to finally try the place. It had certainly *smelled* delicious as she waited for her order to be ready. The cool night air was a refreshing change of pace as she leaned against her car, taking in the scene. A father in his early-forties was seated at one of the nearby tables, having dinner with his young daughter, who was dressed in a mask and red cape. A high school couple sat nearby, splitting a shake and fries. The atmosphere reminded her of something from *American Graffiti*. Even the setting, with the towering Blake's Lotaburger sign overhead, and the concrete picnic tables topped with red, white, and blue umbrellas looked like a place teenagers might have frequented fifty years ago while cruising the strip.

Alex was unwrapping her burger and preparing to take her first bite, when the radio in her car crackled to life.

\\ *"We need an ambulance dispatched to 4202 Saint Michaels Drive for a gunshot injury. Immediate police response is requested by all units. Shooter may still be at the scene, armed and dangerous."*//

For some reason, that house number struck a nerve. Alex dropped her food back in the bag and set it on the roof as she leaned in through her window and turned up the volume.

"Repeat, immediate police response is needed at 4202 Saint Michaels Drive."//

"10-4," an officer radioed back. "That the Greenwood place?"

"That's affirmative. Greenwood is the victim."//

Dammit, Alex thought as she pulled the door open and climbed behind the wheel. She knew she shouldn't have let Luke go over there!

She started the car, shifted it into reverse, and stomped on the accelerator, tearing out of her parking space and sending her burger and shake tumbling down the windshield onto the hood. Then she threw the car into drive and stomped on the gas.

"Shit." She muttered, as she glanced in the rearview mirror to see her dinner tumbling into the road behind her.

Luke dove onto the shag carpet in the master bedroom and crawled around the far end of the bed. From there, he could listen as the gunman entered the residential side of the home. Yet, no sooner did he settle into his hiding place, then the thought occurred to him that it was perhaps the most obvious spot he could have chosen. The first place the shooter was likely to look was behind the bed in the first room he came upon.

The sound of uneven footsteps in the corridor rattled Luke into action. He took a deep breath and jumped back to his feet, crouching low as he ducked into the master bathroom and slipped through another door connecting to Greenwood's den. He pulled the door closed behind him, and took in his new surroundings. The den, like every other room in the house, was engulfed in darkness. The only light came from a wall of windows at the far end, and the dim glow of a computer monitor on the desk, where the Greenwood Renewables logo floated back and forth across the screen.

There was a creak out in the hall, then silence.

The gunman had slipped into the bedroom.

Luke's pulse pounded in his temples as the pressure mounted for him to act.

To the left was a door leading back to the main corridor. To the right was a sliding door to the balcony. Luke padded over to the slider and opened it as wide as possible. The curtains billowed in with the summer air as he leaned outside, studying the balcony that hugged the exterior of the house. If he took that route, running as fast and far as possible, he might find a way down to the ground, or encounter another entrance, where he could duck back into the house and circle around to safety. That was likely his best bet. Unfortunately, he tried to be clever.

Alex made her way up to the driveway. The house loomed menacingly above her as she pulled to a stop behind Luke's Mustang and killed the lights. She could hear ambulance and police sirens weaving their way through the outlying neighborhoods. The muscles in her neck tightened as she surveyed the perimeter of the pitch-black house, weighing the best angle of approach.

A noise clattered from the master bath, followed by silence.

The intruder had knocked something over in his search.

Luke's head whipped around to the corridor exit. He padded across the plush carpet, and slipped out into the hall, pulling the door closed behind him. The moment the door's hinges creaked, he knew he'd made a grave error. He could only hope the sound had gone undetected.

As he hustled down the corridor – toward the stairs, and the house's more extravagant features – Luke pictured his hulking pursuer emerging from the bathroom and surveying the den, his eyes darting toward the billowing curtains at the balcony door, then scanning the room, searching for the source of that distinctive sound…

Luke had just reached the stairs when the door behind him was thrown open as the gunman raged out into the hallway and started shooting.

Alex's eyes were following the lines of the glass and steel balcony when the sound of gunfire echoed from inside the home. The sirens were getting louder now. She looked down the hill to see the lights from an ambulance and two police cruisers turning into the drive.

Bam! Bam! Bam!

Three more shots and her head whipped toward the front door. She pulled her gun from its holster, rushed up the stairs to the front entrance, and ducked inside.

Drywall and glass exploded around Luke as he dove for the stairs, taking the steps a half dozen at a time – less a descent than a barely controlled tumble. He lost his footing as he reached the bottom, stumbling and striking his head on one of the rails. He pulled his hand up to the wound as he got to his feet, and brought it away to see blood running down his palm.

That was going to leave a mark.

Then he was running full tilt through Alan Greenwood's fun-house. Through the pool room, the theater, the bowling alley – alive with blacklights and glowing paint – all the while trying to get as far ahead of this maniac as possible.

Unfortunately, rage had dulled his pursuer's pain. He also seemed to have a better sense of the layout of the house than Luke did. Though it was dark, and though he and Carley had gone on their own self-guided tour of the place, Luke got the distinct feeling that the man barreling through the rooms after him knew exactly where he was going, and had no intention of letting Luke get out of there alive.

Alex held her semi-automatic at the ready as she swept the interior of the house. Two more shots rang out somewhere in the guts of the place. She followed the reverberations down a blue, glass-lined hallway, approaching each doorway with caution, but increasing her pace at the sound of fresh gunfire. The walls near the end of the hall were riddled with bullet holes, cracks spider-webbing through the thick panels. Shattered glass was strewn down the stairs.

Unless Luke carried a heretofore unseen handgun along with his notebook and pen, Alex assumed her reporter friend wasn't tonight's trigger-happy guest of honor. The ongoing gunfire was an encouraging sign that Luke was keeping far enough ahead of the gunman to avoid being hit. Of course, this little game of pursuit was playing out in a large, but ultimately finite maze, and as with most games of cat and mouse, the longer it went on, the better the chances it would end with the hunter cleaning his claws. Luke's best chance of getting out of Alan Greenwood's house alive hinged upon Alex getting to the gunman before the gunman got to Luke.

The balcony that hugged the exterior of Greenwood's home swooped down to the house's lower level at the point where the building jutted out over the twisting driveway below. Luke emerged in the recreation room, a wide-open space filled with pool tables, pinball machines, and countless arcade games. A wall of floor to ceiling frosted glass doors took up the room's far end.

Luke slumped against the doorframe as he fought to catch his breath. He should have learned his lesson the last time a story had put him in this kind of situation; cardio fitness was invaluable. A few less Frito pies and the occasional lap around the Farmington High School track might have upped his chances of survival. With any luck, perhaps his pursuer was wearing down as well. By this point he *had* to be feeling the ill effects of his injuries. That felt like wishful thinking however. So far, the guy had been on Luke's heels every step of the way.

He peered across the room half-lit by the glow of the arcade machines. Red and blue lights were flashing over the frosted glass that separated the rec room from the balcony outside. 9-1-1 dispatch had come through. The cavalry was headed his way. He just needed to avoid catching a bullet long enough to get out to them.

Luke ran across the room toward the flashing lights, arms and legs pumping as he tried to cover as much distance as possible before company arrived. About three quarters of the way there, the squeak of a boot heel told him it was time to hit the deck. He dropped to the floor, sliding under the nearest pool table, and crawling commando-style beneath it to the end, where he paused to see what he was dealing with. A door to the balcony stood about fifteen feet from where he was sprawled out. Luke looked back the way he'd come in, roughly 20 yards away, and watched as a pair of boots slowly crept across the threshold. The right foot came down first, solid and straight. The left foot came in next, the toe dragging slightly before the heel set down.

Luke rolled onto his back, pulling a pool ball from the return slot above him. He looked to the bank of arcade games, where the cool lights of *Pacman* and *Crazy Taxi* alternated with the warm, incandescent glow from the pinball machines. If he could just get out to the balcony, perhaps he could get the attention of someone on the ground. Or hell, if worse came to worst, he could always jump. It would be one hell of a fall, but that beat a bullet to the head.

Of course, crossing the room unscathed was another matter. He watched the boots by the door; the moment they began to move, Luke reached his arm out and started the eight ball rolling across the smooth floor toward the row of game machines. When it was roughly a quarter of the way there, Luke, still out of view, began crawling for the balcony. He was five feet from the glass door when the pool ball bounced off the side of *Pacman,* ricocheting with a clatter. The gunman opened fire, tearing the machines apart in a hail of sparks and shattering glass.

At the height of the chaos, Luke jumped to his feet, threw the door open, and slipped out onto the balcony.

The gunman lowered his weapon as the machines fizzled out and the room once more fell silent. His head jerked to the side as a glint of light off the edge of the door caught his eye.

Alex pressed her back against the wall in the corridor, waiting for the shooting to end. When it stopped, the air was filled with the smell of burning electrical.

So far, she had managed to stay just a few steps behind them, but the gunshots were becoming more frequent. She'd be pushing her luck if this dragged out much longer. If Luke hadn't been hit this time, the chances were good that the next skirmish would be the last.

She slid along the wall, stopping just outside the room from which the most recent gunshots had erupted, straining her ears for any sounds from within. Finally, she heard the sweep of a door opening, followed by the gentle click of its latch.

Alex stepped through the doorway, gun at the ready, and looked across the room to a wall of frosted glass. It curved sharply at its center, the spot where Alan Greenwood's house jutted out at its most extreme point. Through the glass, she could see the silhouette of a seemingly unarmed man on the left side of the balcony, he was crouched over slightly, looking back over his shoulder as one hand held the handrail.

If she was right about the way this was playing out, that figure was Luke.

On the right half of the glass wall, on the other side of the curve, she could just make out a second figure, lurching forward as he moved, as if from a limp. From where she was standing, it appeared neither of the figures could see the other from around the bend in the wall. Not for the moment at any rate, but that would change as soon as one of them rounded that point. If the limping figure got there first, he would have a clear shot at Luke down the length of the balcony.

That assumed of course that she was right about which of the silhouettes was which.

Alex raised her gun, taking a bead on the limping figure as it slowly approached the point of no return.

The number of red and blue lights outside was growing as more and more police and emergency personnel arrived on site. Unfortunately, from down on the ground, none of them could see the scene playing out on the balcony high above them.

Alex tracked the silhouette on the right as it moved steadily forward.

She waited, arms outstretched, sights set on the center of the approaching figure's torso. Her finger held steady on the trigger as she watched for any sign that she might have things backward. She wouldn't get a second chance at this.

The limping figure moved to the left a little further... a little further... til it crossed the tipping point and stopped short. Alex took a deep breath and held it. Then, just when she was on the verge of second-guessing herself, the gunman raised his weapon.

Alex pulled the trigger, squeezing off two shots in rapid succession.

The glass exploded as the bullets hit their target, throwing him to the side, where he slammed into the rail and flipped out of sight.

Alex rushed to the jagged opening, stepping out to the balcony to peer down at the broken figure sprawled on the driveway below. She narrowed her eyes, trying to get a look at the bloody face in the shadows, only to be startled by footsteps in the broken glass to her left. She whipped around, gun at the ready, but lowered her defenses when Luke stepped out of the shadows.

"Thanks," he said. "You got here just in time."

"Didn't I tell you be to be careful? Now you owe me a burger."

Two gurneys rolled past as they sat on the steps. The first held a zipped-up body bag, which was quickly loaded into the medical examiner's van. The second carried Alan Greenwood; an oxygen mask was secured over his mouth and nose, and his body was rigged up to an assortment of equipment to monitor his vitals, all of which were astonishingly strong, given what he'd been through.

"Is he going to make it?" Luke asked the blond-haired EMT who was examining the cut on his forehead. The name badge on her uniform said RACHEL.

"It looks promising," Rachel said as she watched her colleagues load Greenwood into the ambulance and start down the drive, lights whirling. The siren came on as the ambulance reached the bottom of the driveway and headed for the hospital.

"What about him?" Alex asked, giving Luke a nod. "Is he gonna need stitches?"

"It could go either way," Rachel said as she applied the second of two butterfly bandages to the cut near Luke's temple. "Stitches might be a good idea, but it's a fifty-fifty scenario with that type of laceration. It could heal up OK without, but it'll probably leave a nice scar."

"*Nice* like Harrison Ford nice, or Frankenstein nice?" Luke asked.

"Probably more on the Frankenstein side, but plastic surgery is always an option."

"If I want to get rid of the scar?"

"If you're hoping to get into Harrison Ford territory," Rachel said with a smirk as she waved her hand over Luke's face.

"Ouch."

Alex laughed. "Seriously, Luke, did you want me to take you to the ER to get that stitched up?"

"Nah, I'm gonna take my chances on the Indiana Jones look."

"You sure he didn't hit his head harder than you think?"

"If he starts walking in circles, give us a call," Rachel replied as she headed back to the ambulance.

Luke got up and walked with Alex to the front of the house. "All joking aside, how did you know you weren't shooting at *me* through the glass?"

"Honestly?" Alex asked before echoing Rachel. "That was another one of those fifty-fifty scenarios."

"Seriously?"

"OK, *maybe* sixty-forty. I was pretty sure I knew who was who, but everyone makes mistakes, right?"

"That's the least reassuring thing I've heard in ages."

"Would you rather I made something up to make you feel better?"

"*Yes!*"

"I don't do that." Alex muttered as they approached a black car that was parked around the side of the house. A team of police officers was busy tearing the vehicle apart. "The good news is that this guy didn't get away, which gives us a slew of new information to go on."

"Like what?"

One of the officers walked over and handed Alex a sheaf of papers from the glove compartment.

"Like his address, for starters," Alex said as she held up the dead man's registration.

15.

3603 MELROSE DRIVE WAS a one-level, brown house with a sun-fried front lawn, a handful of scraggly bushes, and dingy curtains pulled tight over the front windows. Though it was bookended by a grand-looking home with tall arches on its left, and a friendly, two-story red brick house on the right, the home of Alan Greenwood's would-be assassin had a look about it that seemed to growl, 'Leave me alone.' On any given day that summer, and for *decades* before-hand, it had likely sat unnoticed, baking in the sun, the comings and goings of its lone occupant overlooked by all who passed by.

That was until this morning, when John Knudsen and a select team from the Farmington Police had swarmed the home with weapons drawn, a warrant in hand, and a very heavy battering ram at the ready; a ram which, following a perfunctory knock and announcement of their intentions, they'd used to smash down the front door.

The owner of the home, who was now stretched out in a cooler at the morgue, was Bill Mealy. He'd lived at the same address since the mid-90s. Aside from a drunk driving arrest twenty years ear-lier, Mealy had managed to stay off the police radar for much of his adult life. His booking photo from the DUI showed him as a much younger man, with sickly, pale skin, red rings around his eyes, a sore on his lip, and a general drowned-rat appearance. He reminded Alex of the sniveling crook Michael Keaton dangles over the edge of the roof at the start of the first *Batman* film. Owing to the hard-landing on Greenwood's driveway, it was hard to tell how Mealy had aged in the ensuing decades, but his ending had not been pretty.

Alex leaned against the hood of her car a short distance away, drinking coffee from a Circle K tumbler as she watched the proceedings, which seemed to have gone off without incident. The house wasn't booby-trapped, and there didn't appear to be anyone else living there: no roommates, and certainly no wife or girlfriend. A curious web was slowly coming into focus as the investigation proceeded, but the threads linking the four men ensnared in the situation – the survivor: Greenwood, and the dead men: Jeff Larson, Buck Florquist, and Bill Mealy – remained elusive. At the moment, she was looking at two wealthy, well-connected community businessmen, and two deadbeat losers. Had the more off-the-radar guys been disgruntled employees? Were they Larson's pawns? Was there an additional, yet-unknown player in this scenario?

"OK, detective, they're ready for you."

Alex looked up to see Mike Peterson's familiar face. "Thanks. Good to see you."

"You too," he said. The rail thin officer looked much the same as he had at the scene of the Florquist investigation, only now, his white hair was tucked inside a flat-brimmed blue hat. "Jason Croatto is already inside checking things out."

"What's it like in there?" Alex asked as they started across the lawn to the house.

"I won't lie to you," Peterson said grimly. "This guy was clearly on the downlow for a whole lot of years. It's not a pretty picture. I don't know how we're gonna clean it up."

"Oh?" Alex asked warily.

"The place is *littered* with Schlotzsky's wrappers and Hot Pocket boxes. It's disgusting."

She shot the older officer a confused looked, then laughed. "I thought you were going to say he was a serial killer or something."

"Nah, I get the sense he wasn't charming enough to be a Ted Bundy type. Just a zero-charisma low-life. He did however have some materials around that I think you'll find interesting."

He led her through the front door. John Knudsen met her inside.

"Captain Knudsen," she said.

"Detective Spencer, the place is all yours."

Alex looked around her. There was a sunken living room – largely devoid of furniture – to the left, a hallway to the right, and a drab sort of family room around the corner. Everything was lit like the waiting room outside a funeral director's office.

"Anything I need to know?"

The captain shook his head, "Nothing that jumps out at me, but your lab guy seems to be happy with what he's finding."

"Where is he?"

Knudsen pointed over his shoulder to the family room. "Around the corner. Cut through the kitchen, and there's an office in back of the garage."

"Thanks. I'll just take a quick pass through the other rooms on the way," Alex said as she hooked a right into the back hallway.

Peterson nodded farewell as he and the captain walked out to the front patio.

Alex cruised down the hall past the house's three bedrooms. The first room had tin foil taped over the windows and newspapers spread out over half the floorspace. She hoped that had been set up for a dog, but she didn't want to give it any thought beyond that. The second room was empty, save for a handful of scattered *Star Wars* action figures. The back bedroom held an old, drooping mattress, with a sleeping bag spread out on top, and a dilapidated dresser in the corner.

A door at the end of the hall led back to the family room. Nothing had jumped out at her yet, so Alex cut through the kitchen and out to the garage, where she found a bushy head of hair bouncing around under a workstation.

"Finding anything good?" she asked.

Jason Croatto popped up from under the desk. A contented smile spread across his face when he saw her.

"Oh yeah," he replied, nodding at the bottles in his gloved hands. "We have definitely picked up the trail."

"Evening, folks," Rene said as Luke and Alex took a seat at the Skyliner's bar.

"How's it going, Rene?"

"Not bad. I've been digging your articles."

"Thanks," Luke replied. "This is Detective Spencer, she's actually the one handling most of the cases I've been reporting on."

"Oh really?" Rene said. "Well, nice to meet you detective."

"You can call me Alex."

"Nice to meet you Alex. Things have sure been crazy around here lately. Must be that summer heat."

"That could be it," Alex said.

Rene turned to Luke. "No Carley tonight?"

"She had another business dinner with the new owners."

"Seriously? Those guys need to cut the apron strings soon."

"You would think so, right?" Luke muttered.

"Can I get you two something?" Rene asked, a troublemaker's grin appearing at the corner of his mouth. "A little mother's milk perhaps?"

Luke felt his cheeks warming with embarrassment as Alex turned to him curiously.

"Not tonight, thanks. I'll have a Manhattan."

"Really?" Rene asked, looking openly surprised. "I thought you couldn't handle brown liquor."

"What are you talking about? I can handle brown-"

"I'm just messing with you, man," Rene laughed. "Any preference for bourbon?"

"Makers Mark?"

"You got it. One Manhattan coming right up."

"You know, that sounds good," Alex said. "I'll have one of those as well."

"Two Maker's Manhattans. You got it."

"Are you allowed to have a drink?" Luke asked when Rene had stepped away to fix their cocktails.

"Of course I am," Alex said. "A good cop is never off duty, but let's be realistic, Luke. It's 9 o'clock at night. *Officially*, I am off the clock."

"That makes two of us."

"So, who's Carley?"

"Carley is my girlfriend," he replied.

She nodded, filing away the new information. "How long have you been together?"

"This time, just over a year."

"*This time?*"

"We dated back in high school, but lost touch when I left town. She moved to Albuquerque, got married and divorced, then we both ended up back here and…" He stopped himself. "You know, it's probably not the most interesting story."

"Gotcha," Alex said, seeing he didn't want to talk about it. "Second question-"

"Fire away."

"What, pray tell, is mother's milk?"

Luke picked up a stray coaster, tapping it on the edge of the bar. *"Mother's Milk* is… quickly becoming a very tired joke. One I've done my best not to comprehend."

"I think I know the kind," she said, thinking of some of the hazing bullshit she'd been putting up with since joining the new department. "Say no more. I like this place though."

"Yeah," Luke said, looking around the quiet bar. "It used to be busier when they had commercial flights in and out of the airport, but they still have good food, and Rene is the best bartender in town. His white Russians are delicious."

Alex gave him a little look. "Are those the mother's milk?"

"Yeah, dammit. I suppose they are."

She laughed quietly to herself, not at the joke, but at Luke's almost comical irritation.

"Two Manhattans," Rene said as he set their drinks down. "If you want anything to eat, just gimme a shout."

They thanked him and sipped their drinks.

Alex nodded her approval, then she pulled a manila envelope from her bag and slid the old mug shot of Bill Mealy across the bar.

Luke gave the picture a good look. "What are you, man?" he said in a wheezy voice.

"Excuse me?"

"What are you man?" Luke repeated. "You remember that guy at the start of *Batman?"*

"That's exactly what I thought!" Alex exclaimed.

"This dude looks just like him. Who is he?"

"The gunman from Greenwood's house last night."

"Seriously?" Luke leaned forward to get a better look at the man who had tried to kill him. "The guy last night seemed a lot... bigger than that. That's really him?"

"It's an old photo, but yeah, that's him. The fingerprints and everything else match."

"What's his name?"

"Bill Mealy. We searched his house today, interviewed some of his neighbors and pulled anything we could find on him. Jason finished processing the materials from his house just before I came over here."

"What did you find out?" Luke asked

"The last ten years are a blank. No work. His neighbors never saw anyone other than Mealy around his house, and then it was just when he came out to check his mail or get the paper."

Luke studied the picture as Alex paused to take another sip of her drink.

"How old was he?" Luke asked, interrupting her mid-sip.

Alex briefly lowered the glass to say, "Forty-eight."

She was just about to take another sip when Luke interrupted her again.

"Was he from Farmington?"

"Yeah."

"Born and raised?" he asked as the glass was just touching her lips.

This time, she made him wait so she could take a full, relaxed sip. "Look, how about I tell you what I know. Maybe color in some of major details for you, and *then* we play twenty questions."

"Testy..." Luke observed.

"It's been a long day."

Alex pushed her drink aside and sorted through some of her papers before she started to recap everything she has found out.

"OK, first of all, no he wasn't originally from Farmington. He moved here in 1995. Worked for an oil and gas outfit according to the neighbors. He was with them until sometime around 2000, when we was out of work for a while, then he went to work at the Red Mesa Mine."

"Doing what?"

"Something to do with blasting," Alex said. Seeing Luke's eyebrows pop up she added, "Yeah, we'll come back to that. So from roughly 2001 – 2007 he was working at the mine for a subsidiary of Larson Light & Power. In 2007 he sustains some kind of injury to his foot-"

"That explains the limp-"

"Exactly. And for the next ten years, he was on disability, until that ran out a year ago. After that…" She shrugged. "Our mystery man becomes even more mysterious. But this is where things circle back and the plot thickens."

She slid another picture of Mealy in front of Luke. This one looked to be around ten years younger than the first. It showed Mealy dressed in military fatigues, his hair clipped short, face slightly rounder, and his skin significantly more clear.

"He was in the army?" Luke asked.

Alex nodded. "That popped up when we started punching him into the various databases. He was in the army from 1990 to 1995, during the first Iraq War and for a few years afterwards. Joined up when he was 20, left at 25. Can you guess what he was involved in?"

"Something to do with explosives."

"*Ding ding ding,*" she said as she raised her glass. "That, apparently, is the one through-line throughout his personal and professional lives. So far as we can tell. If it burns or goes boom, Bill Mealy either helped to find it, build it, disarm it, or blow it up."

"What was in his house, the complete fall collection of exploding Samsonite briefcases?"

"Unfortunately, no. It looked like some place Jeff Pepper might have lived in when he was starting Macroware in the 70s."

"I'm not sure what that means exactly."

"Total time warp bachelor pad hovel. *But,* he had a workshop in the back behind his garage. That's where Jason logged all of this shit…" She handed Luke a list of chemicals and technical documents. "All of which happens to cross check perfectly with *these*…" She slid two more stacked sheets of paper toward him.

Luke looked over the pages and raised his hands in surrender. "I have a journalism degree. I don't have a *clue* what any of this means."

Alex pointed from the first sheet, to the second two, and back again. "In layman's terms, *this* is the same as these, assuming you set *this* on fire first."

"And what are these from?" Luke asked, indicating the two stacked sheets.

"Samples Jason recovered from the Florquist and Larson firebombs."

Luke turned to the list of materials documented at Mealy's house. "And polystyrene – whatever – what's that?"

"Tiny plastic beads mixed into the incendiary materials. They give it that burning plastic smell and ensure it sticks to people while its burns. Sort of like-"

"Modern napalm."

"Yeah. How did you know that?" Alex asked.

"Even journalists know a thing or two about the theater of modern warfare-"

"Jason told you."

"Yeah, he was theorizing about it when I stopped by the lab after the Florquist fire."

"Damn," she muttered. "I still hate leaks."

"That settles it though, right? Mealy is the mad bomber. Case closed-"

"I don't know... He definitely had the background knowledge and the skills to build them, but how he got them to their intended targets, assuming they were Florquist and Larson, and *why*, is a whole other question."

"Revenge? Maybe Larson was involved in cutting off his disability payments?"

"But what about Florquist?"

"They could have known each other from way back," Luke spitballed. "They both had ties to Larson and his company. Maybe there was some bad blood."

Alex took a sip of her drink and set it down on the bar, rubbing her thumb in the condensation on the outside of the glass as she turned the question over in her mind. "It just seems unlikely, and a bit too convenient. Fortunately, we aren't on a deadline to solve this thing."

"I'm *always* on deadline..."

"You know what I mean." She narrowed her eyes at him. "This is *all* still off the record by the way."

"Of course it is," Luke agreed. "For now... Let's go back to your suspect board. Who are we looking at?"

"At this point, I think it's safe to say that Jeff Larson and Buck Florquist were not the planners behind any of this, unless they were grossly-incompetent masterminds. That leaves Deanna Haubert and her boys."

"But why would Haubert want Larson dead?" Luke asked. "Her business is dependent on him staying alive."

"There's still Alan Greenwood."

"But that would be another kamikaze puppet master theory,

right? Unless he wanted such an airtight alibi that he was willing to risk getting *himself* killed, it just doesn't make any sense."

"How about this," Alex said. "What if Greenwood hired Bill Mealy to off Florquist and Larson, then Mealy took it upon himself to kill Greenwood and cover his tracks?"

"Is it at all notable that Mealy used a gun for the Greenwood attack, but the other two killings, both of which were successful by the way, used firebombs planted in briefcases?"

"One gives more immediate results, the other lets you set things in motion, independent of time and location," Alex said. "The plant it and forget it technique, versus the look 'em in the eye and pull the trigger method. It makes you wonder if the Greenwood attack was more personal."

"Like the briefcase bombs were work for hire, and the attempt on Alan Greenwood's life was something he wanted to do on his own. Still…" Luke grew quiet as he mulled this over.

"What is it?"

"It just doesn't feel right, you know? Where's the logic? There's a rule I've found helpful more often than not in about ninety percent of my investigative reporting."

"What's that?"

"Follow the money. Who stands to gain the most with these particular people out of the picture? If we can find a place where their circles of personal interest overlap, we'll know we're in the ballpark."

"You think there's still another person out there?"

"I don't see why there wouldn't be," Luke said.

16.

LUKE AND ALEX SPLIT two orders of sopapillas, tearing off the corners and filling the hollow pastries with honey as they traded theories on the separate but seemingly intertwined cases. When the buzz from her Manhattans had dissipated, Alex decided to call it a night.

"I'd love to hang out longer," she said as she pushed in her stool. "But I've gotta get back out there tomorrow."

"You sure you don't want to split the last one?" Luke asked, tipping up the plate to show the last pastry.

"Ugh… thanks, but I'm good. If the booze doesn't get me, the sugar will. Anymore honey and I'll be sick to my stomach."

"Suit yourself," Luke said as he grabbed the bear-shaped honey bottle and bit off the corner of his sopapilla. "I'm gonna stick around and put this bad boy out of its misery."

Alex smirked.

"What?"

"Nothing. Just sort of comical talk from a man holding a novelty condiment dispenser."

"Novelty nothin'." Luke said as he squeezed the bear's belly. "It's manly and delightful."

"OK then. You certainly have me convinced. Be careful getting home, Luke."

"You too."

He watched Alex leave, then flagged Rene down for one last drink.

"Mother's milk?" Rene asked.

Luke gave him a reluctant nod.

Luke finished the pastry and sipped his white Russian as he observed a young couple at the end of the counter. The girl whispered in her boyfriend's ear as she moved closer to him.

Luke sighed and took out his phone, stepping away for some privacy as he dialed Carley's house number.

"Hey, it's me," he said when he reached her voicemail. "I'm just having a drink at the airport. I'll probably be here another thirty minutes, then I thought I'd swing by your place and see if you're back. Hope to see you soon."

He hung up and slipped the phone back in his pocket. This business with the endless work dinners had to stop. It had been ages since he and Carley had enjoyed a regular night out together. Lately, if he wasn't working late to meet a deadline, he was sitting at home by himself, watching Jean-Claude Renoir cooking demonstrations on PBS, and trying not to think about the repairs he should be doing on the house.

Though the primary topics of conversation were murder, mayhem, and charred bodies, it had been a nice change of pace to sit at the bar with Alex, sharing some food and drinks. In a different time and place, he'd probably have asked her out. He loved Carley, he just wasn't getting to spend much time with her outside of work hours. It was getting old! It also didn't help that Alex had that whole Jennifer Lopez *Out of Sight* thing going for her either.

Anyway, there was no sense dwelling on it.

He trudged back to the bar, shooting the canoodling couple a vaguely annoyed look as he climbed back on his barstool.

Rene headed his way, wiping down the counter and casting an eye toward his glass.

"You want another?"

"No thanks, Rene. I'm gonna head out in a bit. See how Carley's night went."

"Detective Spencer seemed nice," Rene observed.

"Yeah, she is. She's about as good a replacement for Mick Gridley as we could have hoped for."

"Cuter too," Rene noted. "No disrespect to the dead."

Luke laughed and shook his head. "I'm sure he would have agreed."

Luke left the bar, sober but out of sorts as he stood on the curb in front, debating whether to go to Carley's place or simply head home. More likely than not, he'd get over there and find she was either still at dinner, or had come back and fallen asleep without checking her messages. He was so preoccupied that he didn't notice the pickup truck parked in the lot across from The Skyliner, and failed to see the driver take his picture as he crossed the street to his car.

It wasn't until he'd pulled the Mustang out of the parking lot and started down the hill that Luke looked in his rearview mirror and saw a pair of headlights blink on at the front of a vaguely-familiar, black F-150.

The hairs bristled on the back of his neck.

He'd been on this ride before.

Luke dropped down a gear and stepped on the gas, watching his rearview uneasily to see if his instincts were correct. The headlights met, then exceeded his rate of acceleration, swiftly gaining on him.

His trusty Mustang was no match for the modern monster tearing up the road behind it. He stomped on the accelerator, mashing the pedal to the floor and sending the engine roaring, but he was steadily losing ground to the truck barreling up behind him.

Luke's eyes darted from the road to his rearview mirror. He couldn't get a good look at the driver, the glare from the passing streetlights kept blinding him.

Was this guy trying to intimidate him or flat out kill him?

The road curved up ahead, twisting to the left, with a deep ditch separating the pavement from the steep embankment beyond. If something were to happen and Luke lost control of the car, things would go downhill *fast*. His best shot at getting out of this unscathed was to prevent the driver from either ramming him off the road, or pulling up ahead and cutting him off entirely.

As he approached the bend, Luke began rolling the steering wheel back and forth gently, steering the Mustang in a snaking pattern down the road. He watched the headlights shifting uncertainly behind him as the driver puzzled over what he was up to. If he could just keep his pursuer off-balance long enough, he might make it to the bottom of the hill, where there would be more traffic, more witnesses, and he would stand a better chance of getting to the nearby Police headquarters in one piece.

For a moment, it seemed his plan might work, but the driver of the truck clearly knew a weakened competitor when he saw one. Luke's weathered and rebuilt Ford Mustang was no match for its battering ram-worthy F-150-brethren. When Luke again swerved over into the outer lane, the driver sped up, closing the gap and moving in for the kill. The hulking pickup smashed into the Mustang's driver-side front fender, blowing out the tire. Luke slammed on the brakes and gripped the wheel, fighting to maintain control as the Mustang skidded into the ditch, crashing into the gravel and rocks with a jolt, and sending Luke smashing into the steering wheel.

The truck continued down the road a short distance before it slammed on its brakes, flew into reverse, and drove back to the scene of the accident. The driver rolled down his window, pulled the stopper from a bottle, and hurled it into the Mustang, where it clattered onto the passenger-side floor, splattering liquid over Luke, who was sprawled across the front seats, knocked out cold. A camera flash popped, briefly illuminating the stretch of empty road. Then the driver gunned his engine and sped off into the darkness.

Luke drifted in and out of consciousness, waking at one point in a daze, the sound of his cellphone ringing somewhere in the distance as he took in the interior of his wrecked car. The second time he opened his eyes, he could feel coagulated blood on his forehead and caked around his nose as he looked up at the star-filled night sky. The final time, all he saw were flashing red and blue lights and the blinding glare of a flashlight as it swept around the interior of the Mustang before settling on his face.

17.

"CAN YOU HEAR ME?"

Luke opened his eyes and found he was staring up at a metal ceiling, one which looked oddly familiar.

"Luke?" Carley asked as she leaned into view.

"Where am I?" he asked weakly.

"You're in an ambulance. You were in an accident coming back from the airport. Do you remember that?"

"Someone forced me off the road…"

Carley glanced to the side, making eye contact with someone Luke couldn't see from his current vantage point.

"That might explain the side of his car," a deep voice observed.

Someone ran a wet cloth over his brow. Luke recognized the EMT who had bandaged him up in Alan Greenwood's driveway. She was cleaning blood from a fresh laceration across his forehead, and nodded reassuringly when Luke met her gaze.

"Rachel, right?"

She smiled. "Yeah."

"We need to stop meeting like this."

"You need to watch where you stick your head."

"Wait a minute," Carley said, raising an eyebrow. "You've treated him before?"

"I have," Rachel replied, running her fingers over the two butterfly bandages. "These were my handiwork."

"When was this?" Carley asked, sounding understandably confused.

Rachel checked her watch. *"Maybe* twenty-three hours ago?"

"I feel like I'm completely out of the loop-"

"That would make two of us," Luke said. "How long was I out?"

"We're guessing an hour," Rachel replied.

"No more than two," the unseen speaker interjected.

Rachel dried Luke's head wound and wrapped his head. "This time, I'm afraid you're *definitely* going to need stitches."

"Can you do that here?" Carley asked.

"Trust me, you don't want me stitching him up, I do lousy sutures. We'll take him to urgent care once the police give us the all clear."

"If you'll agree to it, I'd like them to do a blood draw at the same time," that voice said again.

With some difficulty, Luke managed to lift his head high enough to see a police officer standing at the ambulance's open doors.

"Sir…" the officer began as Luke matched the face with the disembodied voice. "If you don't mind, I'd like to ask you a few questions."

"Luke, this is Officer Mitchell," Carley said.

"Mr. Murphy," Mitchell continued. "I'll be handling the crash investigation. I need to get some information from you."

"Sure," Luke said as he raised a hand to his brow. His head was killing him. "Can I sit up?" he asked Rachel.

Carley looked concerned. "Do you think that's OK?"

"We'll see what happens," Rachel said nonchalantly.

Luke sat up slowly and deliberately, looking from Rachel, to Officer Mitchell, to Carley, before taking a moment to inventory his fingers and limbs. As best he could tell, he still had both arms, both legs, and all ten digits.

"Don't worry," Carley said. "You can still type."

Luke sniffed at the air. He smelled something earthy and alcoholic.

"Sir, were you drinking tonight?" Officer Mitchell asked.

"I had a couple of Manhattans," Luke answered. "And one… white Russian."

"Can I ask over what period of time you consumed those drinks?"

"Around… four hours?"

"Is there anyone who can corroborate that?"

"Yes, Rene, the bartender at The Skyliner, and Alex Spencer with the Farmington Police Department."

"Detective Spencer?" Mitchell was clearly surprised.

"That's correct," Luke said as he watched Carley's expression. If she was jealous, she wasn't showing it. "Detective Spencer joined me for a couple of drinks while we discussed some of the investigations I've been covering for the paper."

"Were you by any chance drinking tequila this evening?"

That's what he was smelling.

"Tequila? No, but now that you mention it, I'm sure as hell smelling that right now."

"That's because you're *soaked* in it," Carley murmured uneasily.

Luke sniffed at his shirtsleeve. She was right, it smelled like he'd just spent a week in Tijuana.

"Any idea how this got in your car?" the officer asked as he held up a mostly empty bottle of Jose Cuervo.

"In *my* car? I have no clue, but I certainly wasn't drinking it."

Mitchell paused, as if waiting for the readout from his bullshit detector before he replied. "We'll talk to the bartender and see if he can confirm the information you've provided. And as I said, we'd also like your permission to perform a draw to check your blood alcohol content."

"That's fine," Luke said.

"Also, if you know where we can reach Detective Spencer at the moment, that would be helpful as well sir."

"I have her number in my phone," Luke answered. He patted his pocket, and was surprised to find it empty. "Where exactly *is* my phone?"

Carley held up a handset with a cracked screen. 'They found this thirty feet from your car."

"Does it still work?"

She swiped the screen to unlock it. "Amazingly, yeah."

"Carley, can you give Officer Mitchell Alex's number? She's listed under S for-"

Luke slumped back. He wasn't feeling all that great again.

"Spencer," Carley said, completing his sentence. She scrolled through the contacts until she found Alex's information, then she handed the phone over to Mitchell who copied down the number.

"Are we all set?" Rachel asked.

"I'm good," Mitchell said as he handed the phone back.

"Then, if there's nothing else," Rachel said, turning to Luke. "Let's get you to the hospital and get that head sewn up."

"I'll take my car and meet your there," Carley said. "I have a feeling your Mustang is going to be out of commission for a while."

She gave Luke a kiss on the cheek and climbed out as Rachel closed the back doors. The ambulance flipped on its light and drove away.

18.

THE SUN WAS UP by the time they left the hospital the next morning and headed to the TJ's Diner for breakfast. In addition to two fresh butterfly bandages, Luke was now sporting a dozen stitches across his forehead, and feeling very much the worse for wear. As expected, the blood test had come back well within the legal limit, but the after effects of the incident remained unsettling. Bill Mealy may have been a goner, but it was clear he had not been acting alone.

"OK then," Carley said as they stopped in the restaurant's parking lot. "Now that we've proven you *didn't* guzzle a half bottle of Cuervo last night, is there anything you'd like to tell me about Miss Spencer?"

"*Detective* Spencer? Just what you already know. We've been comparing notes on some of the cases she's investigating."

"The same cases you're covering in the paper?"

He could tell Carley was suspicious.

"What do you think?" he asked.

"I *think* you haven't been telling me everything you've been up to!"

Now she was beginning to show some jealousy.

"This all happened in the last 48-hours." Luke exclaimed. "I haven't seen you since then."

"It's called a phone, Luke. Or better yet, maybe you could try keeping regular office hours."

"As far as phones are concerned, I called you last night and you didn't pick up!" Luke placed a hand on each of Carley's shoulders as he looked her in the eyes, "Believe me, nothing has been going on that I can't tell you about."

"No? Then why in the hell would someone drive you off the road and hurl an open bottle of tequila into your car?"

"I have no idea."

"OK…" she said, still stewing. "And how in the hell did you manage to sustain not one but two headwounds in the last day and a half?"

"Well, someone at Alan Greenwood's home shot at me when I-"

"Someone shot at you?! Are you serious?"

"Yes, I'm serious! And what's more, Alex Spencer is the reason I'm not dead right now!" He stopped. "You know what… let's get into this over breakfast, shall we? I don't know about you, but I'm starving. Let's go inside and I'll bring you up to speed."

Luke stopped at the entrance and held the door for two older women who were walking out. Rather than saying thanking you, the first woman sneered at him and nudged her companion, who shot him a similar look of concentrated disdain as she walked past.

Luke and Carley walked through the restaurant, becoming increasingly aware of a wave of murmurs as they took their seats in a booth by the window. When the waitress arrived, she handed Carley a menu, and carefully filled her mug to the rim with coffee. Then she tossed Luke a menu, filled his coffee cup half full, and walked away without a word.

"Call me crazy," Carley said. "But I'm getting a distinct persona non grata feeling around here."

"Ya think?" Luke said. "Is it the stitches? I'm definitely feeling more Fred Gwynne than Indiana Jones, but this is ridiculous."

"It's ugly," Carley said, sizing up his headwound with a half-grin. "But it's not Pariah-level ugly."

"Thank you," Luke muttered as his phone's ringtone blared in the quiet restaurant, attracting still more glares. He reached for his pocket, but once again found it empty. "You've got my phone."

"Do I?" Carley asked as she dug into her bag and pulled it out. "Well speak of the devil, look who's calling you."

She held up the cracked screen for Luke to see. The incoming call was from Alex.

He took the phone and answered. "Hello?"

"Have you seen the latest?" Alex asked.

"Latest what?"

"Check out KOB news."

Luke lowered his phone and whispered to Carley. "Pull up KOB's website."

Carley opened the browser on her own phone and pulled up the website for KOB Eyewitness News.

"Well, that answers a few questions," she said when the page had loaded.

"What is it?" Luke asked.

Carley turned the phone around so he could see the top story. Above a photo of Luke sprawled out beside the tequila bottle, the headline screamed:

Star Reporter Under Investigation for DUI

"Someone is setting you up," Alex said, as the weight of the photo and headline began to sink in.

Alex was holding a take-out cup from *Cryptic Grindings* when she arrived.

"How is that?" Luke asked as he pointed to the cup.

"It is *really* damn good."

"That's what Kim told me."

Carley turned to him suspiciously. "Who the hell is *Kim?*"

"Alan Greenwood's assistant."

"When were the two of you discussing coffee?"

"On the phone a while back."

"You just… struck up a conversation about coffee?"

"Yep," Luke said. "We were chatting. It's part of my job, remember? That's how I get people to talk."

"Hmmm…" She seemed dubious.

"Nice to meet you, Carley" Alex interjected. "I've been curious to see who this guy was dating."

"Thank you for coming to Luke's rescue," Carley said.

"All part of the job. Well, maybe a bit above and beyond, but – *WOW!*" Alex did a doubletake as she took a seat and got a better look at the cut on Luke's forehead. "Correct me if I'm wrong, but you didn't look *quite* that bad when I left you last night."

"Yeah, I thought the butterfly bandages were a little understated, so I decide to crash my car and get that 'shovel to the head' look that's so popular these days."

"I'm not familiar with it," Alex said, "but I'd say you pulled it off! Speaking of which, interesting morning. I vouched for you with Officer Mitchell. Hopefully my word and your passing blood test should put you in the clear, but whoever leaked that photo also fed it to any social media accounts that would take it… which is to say *all of them*, so it's out there, and it's taken root. The department will put out a statement to clear you of any wrongdoing, but you know how this kind of thing works, the damage has been done, and it will probably have some long-term repercussions."

"What do you think that will mean?" Luke asked.

"That anything you report from now on will have a whiff of unreliability," Carley observed. "At least with the folks who can't be bothered to dig into it, so, roughly 75% of the population."

"Super. Does that mean I can go on sabbatical?"

"Not even close," Carley said. "Although, God I hope the guys from Puzzlebox don't catch this story."

"Oh, I'm sure they will."

"If there's anything else I can do to help clear things up, let me know," Alex said. "Speaking of which…" She took out her wallet and set it on the table, flipping it open so her badge would be visible the next time their waitress came by. "So Luke, what the hell happened after I left last night?"

Over a couple of cups of coffee, Luke filled her in on how things had played out. "Did you recognize the truck?" Alex asked.

"I never got a clear look at the driver, but one of Deanna Haubert's guys was driving a black F-150 when they came after me at the plant."

"You think it was the same truck?" Carley asked.

Luke shrugged. "I can't say for sure. There are a lot of black pickups in Farmington."

"It's worth checking out," Alex said. "I'll head over to Haubert's place next."

19.

"Yep. He's back. Nope, I didn't ask, but the front of his car is all smashed up, so *something* happened."

Luke sat in a folding chair in the waiting area of Nick's Auto Repair, listening to the shop's namesake proprietor talking on the phone to a friend as he surveyed the aftermath of the Mustang's most recent calamity. No matter how extensive the damage to Luke's car got, or how close he came to getting killed, Nick invariably found Luke's hardships so immensely entertaining, that he'd call one of his buddies on the shop phone as he assessed the scope of the repair job. Whether Nick knew Luke could hear his jovial phone conversations from the waiting area, or whether he even cared, wasn't something Luke cared to consider. The fact was, Nick was the only guy who could keep his old, accident-prone Mustang running.

"Yeah, the engine is probably OK this time, but the frame could be another matter. We'll see... How much? Well... let's just say Cabo is looking like a *distinct* possibility this Fall." Nick let out a guttural laugh, bordering on a cackle. "Yeah, I'll let you know, man. Talk to you later."

Nick emerged from the garage, wiping his hands on a rag, his signature cigar bobbing up and down as he spoke. Luke noticed the caliber of Nick's cigars had improved substantially in the time he'd been bringing his car in for repairs. He doubted the upgrade was coincidental. The next time the Mustang needed to be resurrected, Nick would probably be phoning his friend to book tickets to Havana, so he could start picking his smokes up at the source.

"Well, it's not quite as bad as the last time, but it's gonna cost you."

"How much?"

Nick shrugged. "I can't say yet. It all depends on how the frame is looking once I get her up on the rack."

"But you can fix it, right?"

"Oh, believe me. We're *never* sending that beauty out to pasture."

Now Luke knew the guy was screwing with him.

"You wouldn't want to lose all the repeat business, right?"

"I don't know what you mean," Nick said, trying unsuccessfully to suppress a grin.

"Fine, but I'm gonna need a loaner if you have one."

"I have *just* the vehicle for you, my friend."

"No more food trucks," Luke said, recalling the taco truck he'd been stuck with last time. "In fact, new rule, no novelty vehicles whatsoever."

"Define novelty…"

"I need a sensible car that will let me do my job safely and with some semblance of dignity."

Nick nodded. "Trust me, this baby was *made* for you."

Now Luke's Spidey sense was really going off.

"What kind of car are we talking about here?"

Nick pulled a set of keys from his desk drawer and headed for the door. "It's parked out back."

They stepped out into the blinding afternoon sunlight. Luke shielded his eyes as he peered across the dirt lot toward a massive white Cadillac convertible with a set of long steer horns mounted on the front where the hood ornament should have been.

"Tell me that isn't it…"

"She's a beauty, right?" Nick exclaimed. "Picked her up at auction last month."

"Was this auction in Hazzard County by any chance?"

"Joke all you want, but I thought of you the moment I saw it."

"*Why?*"

"Considering the number of altercations you have on the road, the next time someone gives you trouble, I figure you can just run 'em through with your horns!"

Luke crossed his arms. "Is this really all you've got?"

"I'm afraid so."

"How's the gas mileage?"

"Quite poor." Nick replied.

"How's it handle?"

"Like a tank."

"Can it at least get up some good speed?"

"Yes. Stopping can get tricky, but she moves like a son of a bitch."

"What do you mean stopping can be 'tricky?'"

"Nothing to worry about, the brakes are just a little… reluctant at times. But hey, that's why we have *emergency* brakes, right?"

"Jesus," Luke sighed. "And how long do you think it will take to fix the Mustang?"

"Hard to say. Could be a few days. Could be a couple months."

Luke eyed the car disdainfully. "Well, I already look like some kind of back woods maniac with these head wounds, I might as well have the wheels to match."

"That's the spirit!" Nick said as he slapped Luke on the back and handed him the keys.

Luke looked down at the pink rabbit's foot keychain. Something told him he was going to regret this.

20.

To CALL THE HAUBERT Security headquarters humble would have been an understatement. Deanna Haubert's company was housed in a raised metal trailer that looked like it could either weather nuclear winter, or collapse at any moment. Which was to say, it was either rusted and mud-encrusted to the point of permanence, or subsisting on borrowed time. The sad structure sat at the foot of the Red Mesa, the property's defining feature, and the origin of the mine's name.

Alex rolled up to the building, sizing up an orange Bronco parked near the stairs and a black Ford F-150 parked at the far end. She pulled her car up beside the pickup and got out, subtly checking the semi-automatic pistol in her holster as she looked the truck over. She'd been expecting to find damage to the front grill, or the passenger-side fender, and was surprised to find the body caked in dried mud but largely undamaged. Although she was sure Luke's description of the vehicle that had hit him was correct, she checked the sides of the Bronco as well, finding them similarly mud-spattered but free of any signs of a collision.

Had she taken a moment to drive around the back of the building before stopping, Alex would have found *exactly* the vehicle she was looking for parked just out of sight, complete with a crunched in fender. Instead, owing to a misplaced sense of safety, she climbed the rusted front steps and knocked on the door. When no one answered, she knocked again, reaching down and turning the handle as she did so.

It was unlocked.

Alex twisted the handle until the latch clicked, then she pushed on the door.

"Hello?"

The smell of scorched gun powder filled her nostrils as the door creaked open.

"This is Detective Spencer from the Farmington-"

The words died in her throat as she saw the bodies sprawled around the room. There were four of them. A woman and three men.

The blood was still pooling.

Bile hit the back of her throat as she lurched out the door. She gripped the rusty railing in her suddenly sweaty hands as she took a breath of fresh air and tried her best to exhale slowly. The last thing she needed was to start hyperventilating out in the middle of nowhere.

She'd never met Deanna Haubert, but the odds were good that the victims inside were Haubert and the guys who worked for her.

An ignition rolled over behind the building, followed by the sound of a roaring engine as someone stepped on the gas and sped away. Alex spit the sickly-sweet saliva from her mouth and looked up, a flood of adrenaline washing away the nausea as a second F-150, also black, but with heavily tinted windows, powered up the hillside, kicking up a cloud of dust and debris as it reached the top of the mesa and slipped out of sight.

Alex hurried down the steps unsteadily. The moment she reached the ground, the front of the truck reemerged at the top of the mesa as the unseen driver turned the truck sideways and rolled down the window. Sun glinted off the vehicle's glass and trim.

A gunshot rang out.

Alex dove for the ground as a bullet ricocheted off the railing where she'd been standing. She pulled her gun from its holster as she tried to get a look at the driver, but the glare from the sun was blinding.

Two more shots. Bullets tore into the ground beside her.

Alex made a run for the cars as the crack of a fourth shot filled the air.

A stab of searing pain and a bloom of heat erupted in her left side.

Shit.

She fell against the side of the Bronco, holding her pistol steady as she pulled her free hand up to her side. A dark red plume was spreading across her shirt and down her pantleg.

Another hail of gunfire ripped into the side of the Bronco, followed by the sound of the truck's roaring engine as it came tearing back down the mesa. Alex braced her back against the side of the car as she pushed herself upright with her legs. Despite the screaming pain in her side, she managed to get to her feet with just enough time to peer through the Bronco's windows at the approaching vehicle, catching sight of the smashed in fender as the truck sped up and headed straight for her.

She staggered toward the trailer, aiming for the space beneath its raised platform, and dove for cover under the rusted substructure seconds before the truck smashed into the side of the Bronco, driving it across the dirt in a cloud of dust and screaming metal.

Alex eyed the truck's brake lights as it came to a stop. If the driver backed up or got out and rushed her way, she stood little chance of getting out of there alive. Better to go on the offensive than to dig in or run scared. While the tail lights were still glowing red, she raised her gun and opened fire. The back window shattered as the truck flew into reverse. When she held her ground and kept firing, the driver stopped, changed gears and sped away, steering wildly around the wrecked Bronco, the other pickup, and Alex's miraculously unscathed vehicle.

She waited to be sure the truck wasn't coming back around again, then she crawled out from under the trailer and stumbled for her car, mentally replaying what had just happened. The second F-150 had just the damage she'd been looking for even *before* it smashed into the Bronco. As best she could tell, it also didn't have plates, the driver having wisely covered them, or removed them altogether.

Alex glanced at the trailer's open door as she staggered for her car. The victims inside weren't going anywhere, but if she could make it to her vehicle, maybe she could stop the shooter. She fell into the driver's seat, fumbling with the keys as she started it up. With some difficulty, she managed to shift the car into drive and take off after him.

The pain in her side was growing, and she was starting to feel lightheaded as she stepped on the accelerator and sped down the road, weaving wildly on the gravel surface as Red Mesa disappeared in her rearview mirror.

There was no sign of the truck on the stretch of open road before her, and nowhere for the driver to hide on the periphery. At the rate he'd been going, he could be out to the main road and well on his way by this point. Alex reached her hand across to her side, pressing down on the wound as white spots shimmered in her vision.

There was no way she could make it to town. She needed someone to find her before she bled out.

She took a couple of short, quick breaths, gripped the steering wheel tightly with both hands, and stepped on the brakes. The car skidded to a stop. Sweat was beading at her brow as she reached for her radio's handset, pulling it toward her and pressing the button weakly beneath her thumb as she leaned her head against the headrest of her seat.

The radio crackled…

\\ "Dispatch-" //

"This is Detective Spencer," Alex murmured weakly. "Requesting immediate assistance."

\\ "10-4. Please tell me your location." //

"Red Mesa…" Alex murmured a moment before she passed out.

21.

"Mr. Murphy, I've read your work in the papers, with some trepidation at times I'll be the first to admit, but I'm very sorry for all the hullabaloo in the news. We're doing everything we can to make sure the facts of your accident don't get lost in the haze of fake news."

"Thank you," Luke said as he shook hands with Chief Selleck, the towering head of the Farmington Police. "To be honest, it will probably help my standing in the journalist community if they think I'm a little wilder than I am, but my editor is worried this will discredit my reporting."

"And that was likely the goal," Selleck confirmed.

The chief had arrived at San Juan Regional Medical Center just as Alex was being wheeled into surgery, and he'd stuck around ever since, taking calls in a nearby meeting room and working with his assistants as information came in from the crime scene out at Deanna Haubert's office trailer. The details and gruesome nature of the latest killings, followed by the assault on one of his officers, had left Selleck on edge, and though he maintained a courteous demeanor as he and his team worked to ensure a proper response, it was clear that the event had left him unsettled and angry.

A thin, white-haired officer approached. He was accompanied by a younger, significantly more muscular colleague, with neatly trimmed blond hair and a mouth full of gleaming white teeth. It was clear from their body language that neither of them was entirely at ease around their superior officer.

"This is Officer Mike Peterson," Selleck said. "He and his team will be guarding Detective Spencer, and keeping an eye on you until we can get a handle on who did this and ensure your safety."

"How do you do?" Luke said as he shook Peterson's hand and nodded to the officer who'd arrived alongside him.

"I'm very sorry to hear what happened," Peterson replied. "I've only met her a couple of times, but Alex seems like a nice young woman, and a hell of a good officer. Are the two of you… involved?"

"Us?" Luke asked, feeling his stomach tense up. "No, we're just friends. She's been helpful on a couple of stories I've been pursuing. And…" He wasn't sure if he should elaborate much further on the scope of their ongoing collaboration… "She was looking into the accident I was involved in the other night."

"Is that why she went out there in the first place?" Selleck asked.

"I'm afraid so," Luke admitted. "I had a run in with Deanna Haubert and some of her security guys recently, and I thought one of their trucks might have been involved in the incident the other night."

"Do you have any updates on what exactly she ran into out there?" Chief Selleck asked Peterson.

"Other than four people with their heads blown off? Nothing yet." Peterson muttered. "We're hoping Detective Spencer can fill in more of the details when she comes to."

Selleck looked toward the surgery wing. "Hopefully she'll be out of there soon. I've been waiting on word from the doctors, or for some member of her family to arrive, but I'm itching to get out there and get on this son of a bitch's trail."

"Do you know if she has any family in the area?" Peterson asked Luke.

"I'm afraid I don't. She's never mentioned anyone, so I assume no, but I could be wrong."

Peterson turned back to the police chief. "If you want to head out, we can hold down the fort and call you if anything changes."

Chief Selleck hesitated, then he pulled on his cap. "Please do that. I know I should be staying out of the field, but goddammit, I'm pissed off. Peterson, take care of Mr. Murphy here, make sure he's OK. I'll be back shortly."

Selleck nodded to his officers, patted Luke on the shoulder, and headed down the corridor as his administrative team swirled behind him.

Peterson gave Luke a look. "He's certainly an improvement over what we were dealing with a year ago. But hey, look who I'm talking to," He laughed, realizing Luke was all too familiar with the corruption that had saturated the force until recently. "Luke, this is Calvin Mann," he said, introducing his protégé. "I'm going to be taking turns guarding Alex's room with another officer of my... vintage, but Calvin here is tasked with keeping you safe until this whole mess blows over."

"Like a bodyguard?" Luke asked as he shook Calvin's hand. "You really think that's necessary?"

"Better safe than sorry, right? When someone starts assaulting police officers, it kicks things up a notch. We're already trying to rebuild the force's reputation, it wouldn't do us any favors to disregard an apparent threat and have a journalist get killed."

"*Killed?*" Luke exclaimed.

"Maimed?" Peterson deadpanned. "Would maimed be better? It could happen."

Luke turned to the younger officer. "Keep me safe, Calvin."

"I'll do my best, sir." Calvin replied.

"How does this work exactly?" Luke asked. "You just follow me everywhere?"

"Pretty much."

"Do you ride with me?"

"No, I'll have a patrol car and follow behind."

"Won't that be a giveaway that I have police protection?"

"That's sort of the idea," Peterson chimed in. "We're hoping to act as more of a deterrent than anything else. Ideally, the whole arrangement will prove to be unnecessary."

"Weird." Luke said warily. "Well, if that's your job, I'm about to head out. If anything changes here, will you let me know?"

"Absolutely," Peterson said.

Luke did his best to make small talk as he and Calvin rode the elevator to the ground floor.

"Are you from Farmington?"

"Born and raised," Calvin said.

"Same. You go to Farmington High?"

"Go Scorpions!"

Luke nodded. "Me too. What year?"

"Class of 2014. You?"

"Ugh," Luke muttered. "Let's not get into it. Have you been on a security assignment like this before?"

"No, sir. This is actually my first time in the field."

"You mean with Peterson's team?" Luke asked.

"No, sir. I'm… sort of new to the force."

"Oh. Like, how new?"

"This is my second week."

"That's pretty new," Luke murmured, suddenly feeling a little less safe. "Well, I'm sure you'll do great. For my sake, I hope so."

The elevator pinged softly in the background as the two of them stood in awkward silence.

"Do you know Detective Spencer?"

"I met her briefly last week," Calvin said. "She's tough, but…"

"But what?"

"But really cute," Calvin admitted, his face growing flush.

Luke laughed. "Yeah. She is."

The doors opened on the first floor and they started across the lobby to the parking lot. As they neared the entrance, a handsome, tanned guy in his late-20s approached. He was carrying a bouquet of flowers. Seeing Calvin's uniform, he flagged the two of them down.

"Excuse me, I'm here for Detective Alex Spencer. Do you know where she's being treated?"

"Yeah," Luke began. "She's on the-"

"Why do you want to know?" Calvin interrupted, eyeing the front security counter as he stepped forward.

"I just drove in from Albuquerque," the guy explained, his piercing blue eyes turning in Luke's direction. "I got a call about what happened."

"Are you a relative?" Luke asked.

"I'm her husband," he replied.

"Oh… nice to meet you," Luke stammered. "I'm a friend of your wife's."

He put out his hand. "Cole Spencer."

"Luke Murphy…"

Calvin stepped in after an awkward beat, pointing to the security desk. "You'll need to check in and get a visitor's pass. Then they'll send you up."

"Thanks," Cole said and turned to leave.

Luke watched him go. Though he had no business being disappointed, his shoulders fell a little.

Calvin gave him a knowing look. "Well, that sucks, doesn't it?"

"Yeah, Calvin," Luke admitted. "It really does."

22.

AFTER HE SOLD *THE Aztec Review*, Carley's father used the proceeds to purchase a unit in a senior community outside Santa Fe. That let Carley move from the mother-in-law unit in the backyard, up to the main house. It was still a bit of a sore topic, as she'd been on the verge of moving in with Luke when it happened. Though he wanted to be peeved about their aborted cohabitation, Luke had to admit that Carley's place was significantly more comfortable than the late Mike Murphy's threadbare accommodations. For one thing, her house always had food in the fridge and wine at the ready, not to mention nice *thick* curtains, which she was just about to close when she peered out the window and noticed Luke's loaner Cadillac parked outside.

"Jesus, Luke, I'd have gone for the food truck again. That car is ridiculous."

"Tell me about it, but trust me, it's infinitely better than the tacomobile."

Carley's gaze drifted from the Cadillac's gleaming horns to the silhouette of Calvin Mann's patrol car parked under the streetlight.

"All jokes aside," Carley said as she pulled the curtains together. "I'm glad they have someone watching out for you. It's a shame about Alex. Any word on how she's doing?"

"I think as well as we could hope for. Mike Peterson called from the hospital while I was filing the story about the shooting. Surgery went as expected and she's recovering now."

He didn't say anything about Alex's husband. For some reason, he didn't want to get into it.

"That's good," Carley replied as she handed him a glass of wine.

Luke took a sip, and instinctively drew a hand up to his bandaged forehead. "Is it just me, or has Farmington been sucked into a whirlpool of violent crime?"

"It's starting to feel that way," Carley said. "But on the plus side, maybe it will sell some papers."

"Wow," he said, feigning surprise. "You've become quite the cynical opportunist."

"What can I say? When you're waging an uphill battle, bad news is *good* news ten times out of ten."

"Was that your dad's philosophy when he ran *The Review?*"

"Of course not, but a big news day in Aztec was anytime someone rolled into town with a horse and buggy."

"Come on. There were bigger stories than *that*," Luke pointed to a framed copy of one of *The Review*'s more infamous stories. "What about the UFO?"

"That *did* sell papers, but the general consensus is that the crash was a hoax. In terms of real events, anytime things have shifted in the oil and gas business, print sales have surged. In which case, bad news was good news, and good news was *very* good news."

"People love to get wound up about anything to do with the energy markets," Luke observed.

"Absolutely, I mean, look at everything that's gone down with the solar project. Half our articles for the last six months have been about procedural votes and studies of how it will affect the power plant."

Luke rolled his head back, pretending to pass out. "Don't remind me!"

"You joke, but it sells papers. I was thinking about a series Dad did on the coal mine strike back in the 70s. Some sketchy stuff went down then as well. No firebombs or shootings, but there were some definite intimidation techniques. Bricks through windows. Messages spray painted on lawns. Something happens around here when folks feel their livelihood is being threatened."

"Can you blame them?"

"Of course not, but when it involves the mine and the generating station, things tend to turn dark pretty fast." Carley noted. "And if you look at recent events, a lot of the same elements seem to be agitating at the periphery of some very big changes. Then there are the victims, or would-be victims. Jeff Larson was in talks to sell the plant. Alan Greenwood is ready to put the plant out of business."

"But what about Deanna Haubert?" Luke interjected. "If anything, she wanted to maintain the status quo more than anybody."

"So far as we know. But maybe she wasn't targeted for what she wanted, but for what she knew."

"Which was what?"

Carley shrugged. "How would I know? I'm just trying to come at it from a different angle. If I had to guess, I'd say someone out there is covering his or her tracks to protect whatever pieces they have on the board."

"That could be anyone tied to the Farmington Generating Station, from an investor down to a shift worker. It could be someone at the Red Mesa Mine, or a disgruntled former employee at Haubert's company."

"It could also be a string of people..."

"Or maybe it's all just a series of wild coincidences," Luke said. "But I seriously doubt it."

"Me too. General rule of thumb, when you're dealing with briefcase fire bombs, there's no such thing as a coincidence."

23.

AFTER WEEKS OF WAITING, Luke finally got the call that his car was ready. Though he'd never admit it, he was actually feeling a bit wistful as he drove downtown to pick up the Mustang. He'd grown quite accustomed to the Cadillac. There was something oddly relaxing in seeing the world from behind a set of roaming longhorns. Plus, Nick's loaner car had a much more spacious interior. In the Cadillac, Luke could leave his briefcase open on the seat beside him and still have room to keep a bag of marshmallow circus peanuts or some Lotaburger take-out close at hand. Then again, if he kept the car too much longer, he was going to look like he *was* Boss Hogg, and not just some fool driving the Hazzard County kingpin's vehicle of choice.

The news cycle had slowed down over the last few weeks. Luke and Carley were still pursuing leads, and he was sure Alex and Jason were doing the same, but there had been little in the way of new developments.

After weeks without trouble, Mike Peterson and Chief Selleck had reluctantly agreed to release Officer Mann from his security assignment. Luke was sorry to say goodbye to Calvin, who, owing to Luke's ridiculous wheels, had taken to referring to himself at Roscoe P. Coltrane, but they both agreed his protection seemed unwarranted. Luke glanced in the rearview mirror as he pulled into the lot at Nick's Auto Repair, still half expecting to see Calvin trailing behind him.

His car was sitting in front of the garage, freshly cleaned and waxed and sparkling in the August sunlight. Luke got out of the Cadillac, carrying his briefcase and a half bag of marshmallow peanuts, which he tossed on the Mustang's passenger seat as he headed inside.

"There he is," Nick announced as Luke walked in the door. "The man of the hour."

"I'm afraid to ask, but what do I owe you?"

Nick pulled the invoice from the printer. "You sure you're ready for it?" he asked with a little glimmer in his eye.

"I'm really not. But now is as good a time as any."

Nick set the paper face down on the counter and slowly slid it over to him.

Luke flipped the page face up and sighed with relief when he saw the total.

"Better than you were expecting?" Nick asked. He sounded disappointed.

"Oh yes," Luke replied. He pointed at an emergency defibrillator mounted on the wall. "I was pretty sure you'd need that when you told me the damage. You may need to raise your rates."

"Consider it done," Nick replied.

"I was joking. Seriously, please don't raise your rates. A man's gotta eat."

"That he does, Luke," Nick said as he took Luke's credit card. "That he does."

⤳

Luke pulled out of the lot. The Mustang always handled a little differently when he first picked it up from repairs, but after a couple of blocks, he knew it would feel like home again. A test drive would be a welcome change of pace after the summer he'd just been through.

Since there had been no new incidents, Luke and *The Times* had shifted their focus to the Autumn election. In addition to Councilman Givens' seat, there was some question over what would be happening with Red Haubert's position on the council. After Deanna Haubert's murder, Red was taking some time off to settle her sister's estate, but a chair could sit empty for only so long before voters would get restless and a potential successor would start sniffing around. The hazy futures of the generating station and the mine added a whole new level of uncertainty to the situation, as no one knew if there would be a need for security at either location, let alone whether Haubert Security would extend its contracts under new leadership. Luke was hoping to interview Red later in the week to see if she had settled her plans.

He decided to take Pinon Hills Boulevard back to his place. It would be good to get the car out on an open stretch of highway and really open her up to see how things were running. Then, if anything seemed off, he could just turn around and head back to Nick's.

Alan Greenwood had maintained an uncharacteristically low-profile since the attempt on his life, The Greenwood Project was still set to come online any day now, but with the estates of Jeff Larson and Deanna Haubert in turmoil, what that meant for the legacy energy businesses was anybody's guess. Between the election and the solar rollout, Luke's schedule was likely to get increasingly hectic in the weeks ahead. He glanced at the passenger seat, expecting to see his briefcase open with his planner and editorial calendar spread out where he could see them, but when he looked over, he remembered he wasn't driving the Cadillac anymore, and there was no room to spread out in the manner he'd grown accustomed to.

Luke glanced at the road ahead, he had the entire stretch to himself. He reached over absentmindedly and started fumbling with the clasps on his briefcase. That's when he should have realized something wasn't right. Not only were the catches tighter than he was used to, but they were *both* closed. He released the first latch and checked the road. Then he popped open the second, looking over just as he began to lift the lid. A burst of white light flashed inside the briefcase, and he instinctively swept his hand underneath, flipping it up and away from him. The lid sprang open, spilling a viscous, smoldering wave of fire across the passenger-side door and up onto the Mustang's convertible top, which ignited instantly.

Luke clenched the steering wheel, veering off the road and fishtailing on the gravel shoulder, fighting to maintain control of the vehicle as flames raced across the ceiling above him, filling the car's interior with choking black smoke. He slammed on the brakes, skidded to a stop, and leapt free of the vehicle, scrambling to get away from the heat as lashing flames engulfed the Mustang.

Suddenly aware of a searing pain in his fingers, Luke fell to the ground, rubbing his hand in the dirt to wipe away tiny droplets of the burning substance that had spattered onto his skin.

BAM!

A gunshot reverberated in the distance, and the Mustang's side mirror exploded in a shower of glass above Luke's head. He spun around, trying to determine where the bullet had come from.

BAM!

The sound of a second shot pulled his eyes to a line of red bluffs in the distance. Crouching low to the ground, Luke raced around the back of the car, taking shelter behind the burning Mustang as two more bullets ripped into its side.

By now, flames had engulfed the car, with noxious black smoke belching from the vehicle's burning interior. The gunfire ambush was reminiscent of Alex's run in at Haubert's trailer. When you combined that with the firebomb, this was playing like a list of greatest hits.

A bullet ricocheted off the Mustang's trunk, drawing Luke's attention to the bubbling black paint, and with it, a whole new danger. At the rate the car was burning, the flames were likely to ignite the gas tank well before the gunman ran out of bullets.

Luke searched the area for *anything* that could provide cover. He was a sitting duck out here, with no other cars in sight, nothing but wide open highway in the middle of nowhere. A glint of metal caught his eye about twenty feet down the road. He looked across the asphalt to an identical glimmer on the opposite side. A shallow ditch ran behind him, parallel to the highway. With any luck, the metal he was seeing was a drainage culvert that passed under the road. If he could get to the entrance of the culvert, and it wasn't covered with a grate, and if he had any sort of cell phone reception out here, he might have a chance.

That was two ifs too many.

The flames from the Mustang were beginning to roar.

Luke took his phone from his shirt pocket, clenching it in his hand as he imagined the gas in the tank beginning to boil.

Another gunshot rang out from the bluffs. A bullet tore into the dirt behind him.

Luke took off running along the shoulder of the road. Bullets ripped into the gravel behind him, sending up clouds of dust, and spraying his pant legs with rock chips. He was five feet from the edge of the culvert when the Mustang exploded behind him. He dove into the ditch, tumbling through the weeds and sticker bushes and landing on his stomach in the cracked, dried mud. His eyes darted to the culvert opening.

There was no grate. He could get inside.

He crawled on his arms and legs until he got to the opening and peered down the length of the narrow metal tunnel. A circle of sunlight burned at the opposite end. He pulled himself into the narrow opening and immediately checked his phone's display.

The reception icon showed one bar.

He dialed Calvin's number and listened for the ring through the static.

Calvin picked up.

"Hello-"

The line went dead as the signal dropped.

"Shit."

He dialed again. Waited.

"Luke?" Calvin Mann's garbled voice asked.

"Yeah, Calvin. I'm in a bit of a situation out-"

Three more shots rang out, followed by silence.

"I can't... a word you're..." Calvin's broken voice said as he faded in and out.

"Pinon Hills Boulevard!" Luke shouted. "A gunman has me pinned down on Pinon Hills!!"

The line went to static again as Luke waited to hear either nothing or more confusion. Instead, after what seemed like an interminable wait, his friend's voice came through loud and clear.

"10-4! Sending units your way now!"

Calvin stood alongside Luke and Nick as they watched a flatbed truck bring the twisted, smoldering remains of the Mustang into the shop's lot. Luke's beloved car – Nick's trusty cash cow – had been reduced to a burned out, ruptured shell. The seats were melted and black. The roof was a skeletal wire cage. The pieces of the car itself, those still recognizable as a vehicle and not mere shrapnel, were burned down to bare metal.

Calvin put a reassuring hand on Luke's shoulder as Luke looked over at Nick.

"This has got to be a new record," Nick muttered.

The mechanic looked visibly upset. Luke liked to think it was an emotional attachment to his much-loved convertible, but he suspected whoever had done this had just put a dent in Nick's revenue projections for the rest of the year.

"There's nothing I can do for her this time, Luke. I never thought I'd say this, but maybe you should consider getting something a little more disposable. A car no one likes, like a Tercel or a… Saab. Something that won't break your heart the next time some maniac destroys it."

"There's really no way to save it?"

As if to emphasize the futility of Luke's optimism, a seat spring chose that moment to burst through the charred skin of the driver's seat, tearing through the vinyl with a comic *boing*.

"She's a goner, Luke."

"I'm going to need another set of wheels." He turned to see sunlight glinting from a familiar set of longhorns. "How much to get back in the Cadillac?"

Nick sighed. "I'm going to need a *big* deposit."

Luke's eyes sparkled as he pulled out his expense card. "Consider it done."

24.

"I AM *NOT* RIDING in this car again."

"What do you mean?" Luke asked as he proudly steered the longhorns out into traffic.

"I mean it looks ridiculous," Carley said.

Luke stepped on the gas. "I wasn't a fan at first either, but it's really grown on me. I'm starting to think this car carries some serious cachet."

"Luke, I don't know how else to say this, but it really, *really* doesn't." She slumped down in the passenger seat. "I just hope no one from Puzzlebox Media sees me in this thing."

"Well, now you're starting to hurt my feelings."

"I'm sorry. It's OK if you want to cultivate a Hunter S. Thompson persona, but if people see *me* in this thing, they're just going to think I'm an asshole."

"Ouch."

"Nick really didn't think he could save your car?"

"It blew up! I'm lucky it didn't take me with it."

"Quite honestly, it probably saved your life. The explosion got emergency and police out there faster than they ever would have if folks hadn't called in the fireball."

"That's true. I'll pour out a bottle of motor oil in its memory one day."

"I'm serious. You were lucky."

"I know. I was the guy in the culvert with a sharpshooter taking shots at me from the bluffs, remember? I'm not gonna forget that *anytime* soon."

"Maybe we can track down another Mustang for you," Carley said.

She'd always had a soft spot for Luke's car. Worn and banged up as it had been, he'd had it for just about as long as she'd known him. Close to twenty years. It was hard to picture him driving anything else.

"Maybe someday, but classic Mustangs are getting a whole lot harder to find," He ran his fingers over the Cadillac's white leather dashboard. "In the meantime, it appears me and this baby have still got a few more miles to cover."

Carley took a frustrated breath, inhaling the aroma of burgers and fries as she did so.

"Does it seem at all wrong to you to be driving behind a set of bull horns with three sacks of cooked beef beside you?"

"Not wrong at all,"" Luke said as he patted the Lotaburger bags on the spacious middle seat. "If anything, it feels so, so right."

Carley rolled her eyes. "You're a freak."

"Maybe so, but I also owe Alex a burger, and I didn't want to let Jeff Larson's gift certificate expire."

"The dead guy? Using his gift certificate was a top priority for you?"

"He's one of *many* dead guys, Carley. And yes, as far as I'm concerned, I earned these complimentary burgers with my own bruised ribs."

"What a treat for Detective Spencer to have us barging in on her recovery with some bargain basement fast food that you got for free."

Alex had been out of the hospital for a couple of weeks now. Officially, she was on medical leave, but Luke had spoken with her on the phone a few times during her recovery as they continued to piece evidence together.

Carley looked around nervously as they approached Alex's neighborhood.

"Her apartment isn't in your old complex is it?"

"Nope," Luke said. He knew she was worried about Margo Fisher, his snoopy, flirtatious nightmare of a former neighbor. "It's pretty close though. We'll want to stay on guard."

"Think we could convince Officer Mann to shoot her?"

"Margot?" Luke laughed. "I'm pretty sure he won't do that, but we can ask."

He glanced in his rearview mirror to see Calvin Mann following behind them in his patrol car. Calvin had been back on protective duty since the moment he'd arrived at the scene of the highway shooting, rescuing Luke from the culvert when the police determined the gunman had fled the scene.

"Are you sure we didn't bring too much?" Carley asked as she looked through the bags. "This seems like a lot of food."

"I got enough for you, me, Calvin, Alex, and her husband."

"Are you sure she's married?"

"I didn't imagine it," Luke muttered. "The guy said he was her husband."

"I don't remember seeing a ring on her finger."

Me neither, Luke thought to himself as he turned into the parking lot of Alex's complex. Instead, he murmured, "Only one way to find out."

Luke walked one of the Lotaburger bags back to Calvin's car, handing it to him through the driver's side window.

"We'll probably be in there for an hour or so."

"Sounds good. I'll just be out here, gorging myself on this ill-advised second lunch," Calvin said. "Thanks, by the way."

"No problem," Luke replied as he and Carley started for the apartments.

Luke held the remaining burger bags while Carley knocked on the door to Alex's unit. He did a doubletake when it opened and Jason Croatto popped his head out, his eyes widening at the sight of the takeout bags.

"All right, Lotaburger! I'm starving," Jason exclaimed.

Carley stammered, "Oh, Jason, uh-"

"We didn't bring enough for you," Luke announced bluntly.

Croatto's face fell. "What?"

Luke raised one of the bags. "This is for Alex and her husband."

"Husband?" Alex's perplexed voice asked from inside.

Jason pulled the door the rest of the way open so they could see Alex standing in the middle of the room, wearing sweatpants and a shirt from the New Mexico Law Enforcement Academy. She looked confused.

"I'm not married."

"You're not?" Luke said. "Then who was the guy I met at the hospital while you were in surgery?"

"Oh… That was Cole." She said, realizing what had happened. "He's my *ex*-husband. They called him after the shooting and he drove up from Albuquerque. Apparently, he was still listed as my next of kin. We haven't been married for a couple of years now."

"Why didn't he say ex?" Luke asked.

Alex rolled her eyes. "He has a funny way of omitting that part when he crosses paths with other men in my life."

Luke looked at Jason, blinked, and raised the paper bag. "I brought you a burger!'

Jason's eyes narrowed. "Gee. Thanks."

"How are you feeling?" Luke asked Alex.

"Better. Still sore, but I'm healed up enough to start getting restless."

"You said I owed you a burger, so we're here to make good."

"Thanks," Alex said. "Come on in you guys."

"Nice to see you again," Carley said as she followed Luke in.

The living room was strewn with papers, maps, and laptop computers.

"What are you two doing?" Luke asked.

"It looks like a document deep dive," Carley observed.

"Exactly, right," Alex said as she eased herself into a chair and started to eat. "Please, have a seat."

"What is all this stuff?" Luke asked as he and Carley sat down on the couch.

"Lots and *lots* of paperwork," Jason said. "Files and letters recovered from Bill Mealy's house and Buck Florquist's cabin. Laptops, hard drives, email exchanges. Everything we could get our hands on."

"Along with stuff from Jeff Larson's home and office," Alex added. "Anything his family felt might be useful in solving his murder."

"Family? Was he married when he died?" Carley asked. "I knew he had a few ex-wives, but I didn't think he had any family left."

"Turns out he was in the middle of divorce number four at the time of the accident. Bad for Larson, but lucky for his wife. She stands to make a lot of money when the estate gets settled, so she's understandably interested in seeing this resolved quickly."

Luke looked around the room full of materials. "This is a lot of stuff to dig through."

"You're telling me," Alex said. "This burger is delicious by the way."

"I told you," Luke said.

"Are you looking for anything in particular?" Carley asked Alex.

"Patterns. Anything linking the three of them. The *four* of them if we include Alan Greenwood. Business transactions. Contractors. Mutual interests. That kind of thing."

"What about Deanna Haubert and her guys?" Luke interjected.

"We've got some of their stuff too. Larson's stake in the Red Mesa Mine covers a lot of those bases as well."

Carley nodded in appreciation. "Sounds daunting, but fascinating."

"Carley loves this boring kind of stuff," Luke explained. "It's the old school journalist in her."

"Whereas Luke would rather be out there getting shot at and punched in the face," Carley countered.

"Speaking of which, I see they took the stitches out," Alex noted. "It looks good."

"Thanks," Luke said as they sat down beside Carley. He rubbed the scars on his forehead. "They're still a little itchy."

Carley reached over and scratched his forehead. Then she gave him a little slap on the face. "There there. Your friend got *shot!* You'll be just fine."

"You guys have sort of an edgy, combative thing going on, don't you?" Jason noted.

"Do we?" Carley leaned against Luke. "I guess that's the hazard of romance. Which reminds me, is the wife a suspect?"

"In Larson's killing? She could be, but it's hard to see how her interests fit with the other attacks," Alex said.

"Clearly Bill Mealy didn't have the market cornered on pyrotechnic briefcases," Luke observed. "If he did, I'd still have a car."

"And unfortunately, whoever was behind the latest incident is still out there somewhere," Alex added.

"Hopefully some detail in all of this will help us figure out who they are, and why they're doing this." Jason said.

Carley leaned down to get a better look at some of the paperwork fanned out on the floor. "Do you mind if I take a look?"

"Have at it," Alex said. "We could use a set of fresh eyes."

Carley scooped up a pile of pages and started sorting through them. There were email printouts, business filings, company statements regarding the solar installation, and possible targets for the sale of the existing coal plant.

"Bill Mealy was ex-military," Alex said to Luke. "Looking at the way you were targeted, it appears to fit the same pattern, which means any and all correspondence originating from Mealy's home could be a potentially rich source for leads. We're looking for people with sharpshooting experience and explosives training. We're also digging into a group of investors that has spearheaded attempts to purchase the Farmington Generating Station in order to market its output to neighboring areas when The Greenwood Project comes online. There could be any number of potential avenues where that's concerned."

"Almost too many," Jason explained. "But so far, they've done a very good job concealing just who exactly they are."

"So the field of suspects is still wide open," Alex added. "It's going to take some time to narrow things down."

Luke looked at Carley, who was already immersed in the paperwork.

"It just so happens that we have some time free this afternoon if you want some help."

"Then please," Alex said, waving towards the papers. "Dig in."

25.

"You may see me as a businessman, but I'm *really* just a dreamer."

Luke was just entering the packed Farmington Civic Center when he heard Alan Greenwood deliver his signature proclamation. Had Carley been with him, he'd have shot her one of his signature eye-rolls. Instead, he looked to either side and saw people clapping and smiling. Even after all the protracted negotiations and halting progress on The Greenwood Project, Greenwood had the crowd eating out of the palm of his hand.

Luke peered around the auditorium, taking in the scene. His adrenaline was still up after what had happened on his way there.

"I'm gonna go on ahead," Luke said into the speakerphone as he knotted his tie.

"Luke, man, I am on my way. Just wait a few minutes. I'm two blocks from your house."

"Calvin, it will be fine." He grabbed the rabbit's foot keychain and started for the door. "I'll meet you in the lot across from the center. No one is going to bump me off in the next ten minutes. If anything, Alan Greenwood is tonight's top target."

It was starting to get dark as Luke passed Sacred Heart Church and *The Times* building. He couldn't tell for sure under the glare of the overhead streetlights, but a few blocks from his destination, he thought he spotted a familiar black truck pulling out in front of him. Luke eased off the gas to allow some distance between the two vehicles. With any luck, the driver's eyes wouldn't be drawn to the flashy set of longhorns creeping up behind him. As the pickup took a right, it looked as though the passenger-side fender might have some damage. Luke turned onto the next street as well, but to his surprise, when he rounded the corner the truck was nowhere to be seen. Luke slammed on the brakes as he approached a nearby alleyway. After a moment's hesitation, he cranked the wheel to the right and headed down the trash-strewn back corridor. He immediately realized it was a dumb decision. Not only was the truck nowhere to be seen, but the massive Cadillac was practically scraping its horns on the fences and walls that bordered the alley on either side.

Perhaps Carley was right. Maybe this car *was* a bit ridiculous.

He crept along slowly, looking to the left and right to see if the pickup had pulled into a parking spot or garage on either side. By the time he reached the end of the alley and reconnected with the street, Luke wondered if he'd let his imagination get the better of him.

His heart nearly ricocheted out of his chest when a police siren squawked at him from the intersecting street and Calvin Mann called to him from the loudspeaker on top of his patrol car.

"What are you doing?"

Luke scowled, his heart still pounding as he pulled out in front of Calvin and continued on to the civic center. News crews and satellite uplink trucks lined the block, with cables snaking across the sidewalk and into the building. Security guards were stationed at every doorway. Luke turned into the lot across from the civic center, parking next to a silver 1976 Oldsmobile Cutlass.

Calvin pulled up beside him and rolled down his window. "Did you see something back there?"

Luke shook his head. "My mind was playing tricks on me."

"You want me to go in with you?" Calvin asked.

"This place is already swarming with security," Luke said.

"You're probably right, but I'll stick around just in case." He nodded at the longhorns. "Make sure no poachers mess with your ride."

"Thanks," Luke replied as he started across the street.

He was running late. Other than security, most of the remaining people outside the Center were crew members for the various broadcast outlets covering the event. The incidents surrounding the shuttering of the Farmington Generating Station and the Red Mesa Mine, along with the attempt on Alan Greenwood's life, had turned the evening's festivities into a national story. The coverage from tonight's event would no doubt be going out nationwide. Luke was merely a hometown small fry, in a basket of primetime potatoes. Unfortunately, the buzzcut-sporting security guards at the main gate were locals.

"Luke Murphy," Buzzcut Number One said as he examined Luke's ID and checked his name on the guest list. "You're late."

"Yeah," Luke said impatiently as he heard the roar of the crowd swelling inside.

"No outside drinks are allowed in the facility," Buzzcut Number Two said with a smirk.

"You'll need to check your tequila with us for… safe-keeping," His friend chortled.

"Nice one, guys," Luke muttered as he headed inside.

"Ladies and gentlemen," the emcee announced, the words booming from the auditorium's double doors as Luke raced through the reception area. "This evening, I have the honor of introducing one of Farmington's most notable and revolutionary public citizens. A man who has shaped this city in ways big and small, and who, tonight, will set us on our course for the future, by rolling out one of the biggest solar installations in not just the country, but around the world."

Luke flashed his press credentials at the doors and slipped into the jam-packed audience, swerving back and forth through the oncoming crowds.

"Without further ado, I give you Mr. Alan Greenwood!"

Luke craned his neck to see Greenwood, in the motorized wheelchair he'd been using since the attack, rolling out from behind the curtain and stopping before a lectern at the center of the stage. When he rose from the chair and stepped toward the microphone, the crowd completely lost its mind.

"Thank you, ladies and gentleman," Greenwood began. "This is a very special night for me. One I wasn't entirely sure I'd be around to witness!"

The crowd laughed knowingly.

"But your letters and words of support kept the dream alive. It's been a long haul these last few weeks, and an even longer haul in the months and years leading up to today. But thanks to all of you, we are about to take the City of Farmington into the future!"

Greenwood paused for a sip of water, then he took a slow, deliberate look around the room. He pressed his fingertips together and waited.

"Ladies and gentleman, you may see me as a businessman, but I'm *really* just a dreamer."

The audience went wild again.

"And one of my biggest dreams is about to come true."

The curtains behind Greenwood parted, revealing a towering screen. A video image faded into view behind him as the lights in the auditorium dimmed. The live view from an aerial drone pulled into focus as the camera raced over the desert landscape outside the city. The unmistakable light from a southwest sunset filled the screen. Suddenly, a sea of solar panels came into view, and the drone slowed its flight, hovering and circling around the glimmering facility.

"Construction is now complete on The Greenwood Project, one of the largest solar facilities in the United States. Powered entirely by the sun, the project uses 1.75 million monocrystalline silicon modules to produce enough electricity to power more than 260,000 households. That's enough electricity to power every home in Farmington, as well as all of the city's public buildings, streetlights, medical facilities, schools, and other infrastructure, with plenty more to spare. In short, complete, *sustainable* energy independence for the city of Farmington. Not too shabby, right?"

The crowd hooted and hollered. Then the image behind Greenwood split in two, with one side holding on the solar facility, and the other fading to a silhouetted image of the generating station, where clouds of smoke and steam were pumping into the air. A smattering of boos echoed from the back of the auditorium.

"You're all familiar with the Farmington Generating Station," Greenwood continued. "Some of you have perhaps worked there. I'm certain you've *all* paid a bill or two from them over the years. Well, the generating station is about to enter the next phase of its history, one separate from the City of Farmington. New ownership will be taking over shortly to pursue *their* dreams, while the Greenwood Solar Project leads Farmington down the road to the future."

More cheers as Alan Greenwood stood before the split screen image of The Greenwood Project and the generating station. He held his hands out to the sides like a conductor preparing to lead his orchestra.

"We have traveled a great distance to get here, with many delays and challenges along the way. The initial plan was to power up the facility, ready the plant to go offline, and make the switch over one week from today, but our plans have been changed," the crowd gasped. "Instead of next week, we will be making that switch… tonight."

More excitement and camera flashes as applause filled the air. Greenwood smiled and laughed as an oversized prop handle was wheeled out onto the stage. He crossed the stage, limping slightly as he swept his hands up in the air, urging the crowd to cheer louder and louder.

"Don't ask me how this all works. I leave the logistics to my team, but as I understand it, the projector and all of our presentation equipment are on battery backup, while the auditorium lights, and everything else around us is coming straight from the grid. We've had the panels up and running for the last few weeks, tucking away energy for just this moment. When I pull this handle, we'll be able to watch in real time as the Farmington Civic Center, and everything in the city makes the jump to one hundred percent renewable energy."

Greenwood seized the handle with theatrical aplomb. He slowly pulled it down until it clicked into the place in the middle. The live images on the screen remained, but the lights in the auditorium grew dim, then blinked to black. Greenwood pressed the handle the rest of the way down, until it locked into place at the bottom. The onscreen image of The Greenwood Project swelled, along with a dramatic humming sound, as the lights in the auditorium grew increasingly brighter, until they were once more fully illuminated.

Luke couldn't help but clap his hands along with the crowd as Alan Greenwood took a bow on stage, basking in the excitement.

After the presentation, members of the press were ushered backstage for a question and answer session with Greenwood himself. Luke joined the swarm of reporters, but stood at the back of the room, observing the proceedings without throwing out his own inquiries; he'd had more than enough access to Alan Greenwood to seek all the answers he was ever likely to get. Mostly, he just wanted to hear what the national news outlets hoped to learn from Farmington's quirky, daydreaming benefactor.

The revelations were few and far between, primarily soundbites and various bob and weave variations of the "just a dreamer" mantra. After less than twenty minutes, Greenwood thanked them for coming, returned to his motorized wheelchair, and rolled offstage.

Afterwards, as the temperature in the room began to climb, and the line at the main entrance backed up with little indication of clearing, Luke slipped out a side door, and found himself alone in a dimly-lit hallway lined with framed black and white photographs. There wasn't a soul around. He glanced at the images as he walked uneasily through the silent corridor, his footsteps echoing in the silence.

The image of the black truck flashed in his mind as he rounded a corner and found himself in a long, unlit passageway, with a set of stairs at the far end. Light filtered down the distant steps, which he *hoped* led to a more heavily-trafficked section of the civic center. Luke's sense of direction was usually fairly good; if he had to guess, he expected to emerge in the main reception area outside the auditorium where Greenwood had presided over the impromptu changeover from coal power to solar energy.

He started down the corridor, walking slowly and deliberately at first, but increasing the pace as his imagination began to get the better of him. Somewhere in the darkness, he heard what sounded like shoes squeaking on the hard floor. A set of keys dropped, followed by a door slam, and Luke took off running, glancing over his shoulder as he sprinted down the corridor.

He reached the stairs, skipping the steps one and two at a time, and almost falling as he pivoted on his foot, caught himself, and collided with one of the very last people he'd ever have expected to see at the night's event.

"Careful, Luke," Councilman Givens laughed as he caught Luke's shoulders and steadied him. "Why the mad dash?"

"Councilman..." Luke said, his cheeks flushing with embarrassment.

"Where are you headed in such a hurry?" Givens asked.

"Just getting back to file my report," Luke gasped. He was feeling winded.

"You realize you're working for The *Daily* Times, not the *New York* Times, correct? There are very few stories around here that are worth getting killed over. There's certainly no need to be running yourself ragged."

"It never hurts to set high standards, right?" Luke said. "What are you doing here anyway? Aren't you a solar energy skeptic?"

"I haven't been all that excited about The Greenwood Project," Givens admitted. "But it's a new age, right? I might as well get on board."

"Plus, it's still an election year," Luke observed. "And solar is popular, correct?"

"There's that too." Givens deadpanned as his gaze drifted to the row of TV cameras lined up outside.

Luke could practically hear the political gears grinding in the councilman's head. "Listen, don't let me hold you up," Luke said. "I've already turned in my campaign coverage. You might as well talk to the big boys."

"Well, OK then." Givens said. "But only if you insist, Luke."

Luke watched the councilman head out to talk to the press, then he stepped outside as well, giving the TV crews and Givens a wide berth as he crossed the street and returned to the Cadillac.

"Anybody mess with my ride, Calvin?" Luke asked before he unlocked his car.

"Unfortunately, no," Calvin replied as he eyed the longhorns.

26.

Luke was daydreaming about Kay's death when the letter arrived.

In his defense, she *had* been snapping her gum especially loud that morning. Of course, he and Carley had also been up late the night before, bickering about her work hours, which didn't help matters. Carley was set to have her 'last state of the acquisition' meeting with the Puzzlebox Media guys over breakfast the next morning, so she was understandably nervous. Luke really didn't have a leg to stand on with his complaints, he knew she was under pressure and that she couldn't really tell her new bosses to piss off, but the fact was, he was bored and lonely, so he was doing what any guy would do in that position: acting like a petulant ass. A man can only spend so many nights alone, ignoring home repair projects, before he needs some companionship. So, when his girl-friend finally came over for the night, his primitive mind decided that was the *ideal* time to make a few passive aggressive comments so they could spend the rest of the night arguing.

It seemed like a great idea at the time.

Fortunately, Carley was smarter than he was, so they had even-tually come to a sort of truce, ending the night on a peaceful note.

Of course, this morning they were both completely exhausted. Now she was off at the business breakfast while Luke was slumped at his desk, going over a story as the gossip columnist in the next cubicle sorted through her mail, happily snapping her gum and talking to herself.

"Oh Peggy Sue, you old so and so…" Kay muttered as Luke ran spellcheck.

Each comment was accompanied by the crack of gum as Kay bit into a bubble and scoured the next letter sent in by some neighborhood busybody. Every time Kay snapped her gum, Luke knew she'd pinpointed a new bit of gossip.

Luke rolled his eyes and looked at his watched. It was still too early for a Frito pie and another cup of coffee at the Five and Dime.

Kay giggled. "Land's sakes Brett, just keep it in your pants."

Luke was just about to jump up and trigger a workplace sensitivity workshop, when Kay leaned over the wall, holding out an envelope and smiling.

"Honey," she said. "This one is for you."

"Thanks, Kay," Luke murmured, forcing the biggest fake smile he could muster.

The letter was addressed to:

Luke Murphy

c/o The Daily Times

There was no return address.

Luke took a seat at his desk, running his fingers over the edges, feeling for every reporter's worst nightmare: Any sort of loose powder folded into the envelope. Satisfied that it was clean, he slipped an opener under the edge, sliced the letter open, and carefully unfolded it on his desk. A shiver rippled through his body when he read the first line:

By the time you read this, I'll be dead.

"What is it, something juicy?" Kay asked.

"I'm uh, I'm not sure," Luke said. "I'm gonna need some time to process it."

Kay disappeared behind the divider as Luke continued reading the letter. He had just gone through it a second time when he looked up and saw Carley returning from her meeting. There was a spring in her step that Luke hadn't seen in ages.

"How did it go?" he asked as she stopped by his desk.

Knowing the town's premier gossip columnist was in the next cubicle, they did their best to keep their voices down.

"I'd say it went surprisingly well. They're happy and say the trends are moving in the right direction. So yeah, it's good, I think they're going to step back more and let us do this our way for a while."

"What about me?" Luke asked.

"What about you?"

"Did they say anything about my stories? Personally, I think I've been on fire."

"Oh yeah, most definitely," Carley said, nodding overemphatically enough to let Luke know, he was delusional. "But seriously," she said, lowering her voice a little. "They seemed very happy. They even mentioned the P – word."

Gum snapped on Kay's side of the wall.

"Private offices?" Luke asked eagerly.

"Performance bonus," Carley whispered.

"Well, that's almost as good. How should we celebrate?"

"I have some ideas. Stay tuned."

"Oh, by the way," Luke said as he handed her the letter. "Something interesting arrived while you were out."

Carley took one look at it, and motioned toward her office.

"I have been following your stories in the paper," Carley read aloud from the letter. "Some of the folks you've covered are real sons of bitches, but I am the missing piece."

She looked up, giving him a skeptical look. "My bullshit detector is going off here."

"Mine too, but I guess there's only one thing to do..."

"Should I call her, or should you?"

"It's probably more of an editor-in-chief decision," Luke said. "Do your best Ben Bradlee."

Carley picked up the phone and dialed Alex's number. "Yeah, we have something here you might want to see." She covered the mouthpiece and whispered to Luke, "Forget Ben Bradlee, I'm Katharine Graham."

Though the envelope had no return address, the letter inside ended with a scrawled signature and the location of its author's supposed home, which John Knudsen and his team surrounded as soon as the order went out.

It was an eventful start to Alex's first day back from medical leave. She stood outside the home, conferring with Jason and Mike Peterson as John Knudsen and his team assessed the situation before breaking down the door and swarming the building.

"It's not pretty in there," Peterson told Alex and Jason shortly after he exited the house. "That guy had been dead for at least a week."

"Cause of death?" Jason asked.

Peterson pantomimed a rope around his neck. "Hung himself."

"Are you sure it was suicide?" Alex asked.

"Well, that's for you guys to decide. I don't claim to be Columbo, so I'm sure there are ways it could have been set up to appear like a suicide, but to my eyes, it looks pretty straight forward."

"Knudsen's guys know not to touch anything right?" Alex confirmed.

"I'm a nice guy, so I won't let Knudsen know you asked that. But yeah, detective, we know not to the disturb the crime scene, this isn't *'Police Academy.'* We're professionals. But like I said, he's been in there for a while now. And it's been hot. That place is smelling pretty rank."

"That's not a problem," Alex joked as she patted Jason on the shoulder. "I'll be sending Croatto in to document everything, anyway."

Jason's brow furrowed. "Thanks."

As if on cue, a couple of Knudsen's guys emerged from the building, coughing and gasping for air.

"We need to get some ventilation in this place!" the officer shouted. "Can we open up the garage?"

Peterson turned to Carley. "Any problem with that?"

"Nah, go ahead," she said.

Peterson gave his guys a thumbs up.

A moment later, the garage door at the front of the house began creaking and groaning as it rolled open, revealing a black F-150 parked inside. Alex's eyes locked onto the pickup's damaged passenger-side fender.

"Recognize him?"

Luke stared at the black and white photo Alex had called them down to see. He, Carley, and Alex were gathered in Jason Croatto's lab, surrounding a table covered with evidence, including an old booking photo of a gaunt, middle-aged man with a bald head and intense eyes. One side of his face drooped noticeably.

"I've definitely seen him somewhere before," Luke said. "But I can't figure where."

"He worked at the power plant…" Alex noted.

Luke immediately recalled the face looking down at him from the catwalks.

"That's it. I never spoke to him, but I saw him there the day Haubert's guys beat the shit out of me."

"That's the guy who sent Luke the letter?" Carley asked.

"Apparently, so. What he was doing working at a power plant for the last ten years is beyond me. Yet another former military guy who checks off all the boxes. Experienced sharpshooter. Apparent connections to Bill Mealy *and* Buck Florquist. An assortment of axes to grind-"

"How do you know that?" Luke asked.

Alex pulled a folder from beneath her arm. "His house is a virtual treasure trove of correspondence and paperwork. Florquist's name is in there. Mealy's. There's even some mention of Haubert's security company. And there's plenty more where that came from."

"I'm still going over everything we pulled from his residence," Jason explained. "It's going to take some time to examine his laptops and phone, go through all the hard drives and check his emails and web history for anything that might be of help to us."

"You think this guy was working with Mealy?" Carley asked Alex. "To what end?"

"That remains to be seen, but it's the most obvious theory at this point. They were both set to lose their jobs. Both a bit… off. It's not hard to imagine a couple of disgruntled long-term employees with similar backgrounds egging each other on after hours, coming up with an idea to send a few incendiary F yous to the guys in power."

"Then what? The surviving perpetrator let his conscience get the better of him?" Carley spitballed.

"But only after he tried to set yours truly on fire as well," Luke pointed out. "I just don't know, it seems like this guy... what's this guy's name anyway?"

"Dub Taylor," Alex said.

"Doug?" Luke asked.

"*Dub.*"

"Dub Taylor," he repeated. "That is one *weird* name."

"You'd be surprised how often it comes up actually," Jason said.

"*Dub.* Really? Wow."

"Moving along people," Carley interjected.

"Sorry, OK, so Dub Taylor and Bill Mealy came up with this plot together. One or both of them carried it out. Then, after Mealy was killed, Taylor decided to wipe away all the evidence? But at some point, after he tries to kill me, he starts to feel guilty, so he mails me a letter and kills himself. Why would he try to kill me, then send me a complete confession?"

"Maybe he figured, if you can't beat 'em, join them," Jason mused.

Luke answered the suggestion with a skeptical smile and silence.

"Too neat for you," Carley noted.

"Kind of, yeah. The only thing missing is a pretty little bow on top. It's one step removed from 'The Mobster did it with a banana in the greenhouse.'"

"You've never played *Clue* before have you?" Alex noted.

Luke laughed. "No. No I haven't. My point again is just that it seems too convenient, all the threads pulling together perfectly."

"Sometimes that happens," a deep voice behind them said. "Especially in *Clue.*"

They turned to see Chief Selleck standing in the doorway.

"Detective Spencer, I was just stopping by to congratulate you on a successful operation your first day back," Selleck nodded at Luke and Carley. "I didn't realize we had such a cozy working arrangement with the press…"

"Chief Selleck," Alex said nervously. "Actually, this morning's tip came from a letter sent to *The Daily Times* offices. Luke Murphy and Carley Parker alerted us to it as soon as it was received."

"Thank you for that," Selleck said. He turned to Luke. "Speaking to your concerns, I've been in law enforcement for most of my life, and you'd be surprised how often that happens. People say the world is poised for chaos, but I've always felt the opposite. Unless it's part of their business model, criminals don't thrive in chaos. Uncertainty eats at them. I've had people get away with the perfect crime, they murder their husbands, collect the life insurance, and run away to the Bahamas. But ten, fifteen years later, they need that resolution, so even though they got away with it all, they reach out to the police, and they confess. It sounds crazy, but it happens all the time."

"Maybe you're right," Carley said. "But as an editor, I need to be sure."

"I know, Ms. Parker. I do as well. I *also* know that citizens crave the status quo. Members of the community feel safer when they believe chaos has run its course. It's the best way, perhaps the only way, for people to move forward." Selleck glanced at the photo of Dub Taylor, shook his head, and patted Alex on the shoulder. "Keep up the good work detective. I'm expecting great things from you. And thank you again to *The Times* for helping us let the people of Farmington feel safe again."

"Thank you, sir," Alex murmured as she watched the police chief stroll out of the room.

"OK," Luke said after an uncomfortable moment of silence. "What just happened?"

"I think he was asking us to close the book on this one," Alex said.

"How?" Luke asked. "Do we just run a story and pin everything on Taylor?"

"I'd like to feel more certain about things," Carley said, "But yeah, that's the impression I got. He wants people to read that the worst is over. No more fire bombs and shootings and fear."

"Do you actually want me to write that?" Luke asked.

"Of course not," Carley said. "We'll start with a just the facts report on Dub Taylor and the discovery of his body."

"That I can do," Luke agreed. "Then what?"

"While you're detailing the facts," Alex said. "The three of us will go through everything we have here, and see if we've missed anything that could affect the way the facts relate to the *truth.*"

"Sounds good." He turned to Carley. "Just do me a favor, will you?"

"What's that?" she asked.

"Try not to stay here *all* night."

One root beer float, two Frito pies, and three hours later, Luke was hunched over his laptop in a booth at the Five and Dime, hammering out the final details of his story.

"For the record, I knew from the beginning you weren't drunk when you crashed that car of yours," Betty said as she came by with his bill. "I told my neighbor, 'Mike Murphy's boy has been wrecking that car of his since he first got his license.' You're just a rotten driver is what I said."

"Gee, thanks, Betty."

"I said, 'Randy' – My neighbor's name is Randy. I said, 'Randy, his blood sugar was probably all out of whack and he lost control of his car. You should see how he eats. Sugar and carbs. Sugar and carbs.'" She motioned toward his plate. "I do worry about you and diabetes, kiddo. I mean… Do you still eat those marshmallow circus peanuts?"

"I do."

She shook her head and motioned to the pharmacy section on the other side of the divider. "You know, I saw we have those diabetes socks on sale right now. I don't know what they do, but maybe you should pick up a pair."

"Thanks, Betty," Luke said, hoping to get back to work. "I may do that."

"Say, what happened to that nice police officer who's been coming in with you lately?"

"Calvin? He's been reassigned," Luke said. "His boss thinks whoever was trying to kill me isn't trying to kill me anymore."

"That's too bad," Betty said. "Now *that* young man knew how to eat properly."

She gave Luke a pat on the shoulder and headed back to the counter.

Well, at least the push to clear his name was getting out there. Clearly Betty wasn't on the bleeding edge of the push-back however.

Luke read over what he'd written. As they'd discussed, it reported just the facts regarding the discovery of Dub Taylor's body. There were a few threads connecting the dots from Taylor to Mealy, Larson, Haubert, and the Greenwood assault, but that was largely it. If the head of the Farmington Police was hoping the paper would close the book on the more sensational aspects of the criminal chaos that had enveloped the city over the last few months, he would likely be disappointed. But to Luke's eyes, and his own sense of between the lines messaging, the story largely read like a final chapter, albeit, one that might leave the more closure-seeking reader looking for more.

"Yeah, I just finished," Carley said into her phone as she looked Luke's story over on her laptop. "It's fine. I'm not wild about it either, but we'll stick with it for now. Go ahead and send it to layout with my OK. If we get it to them now, we can still make the morning edition. Yep, I'll see you soon."

She hung up the phone and returned to the website she was using to cross reference web and email addresses from Taylor's computer.

Jason and Alex were ready to call it a night, but Carley was enjoying getting into the weeds of the deep dive. Luke was right, she did revel in the elements of reporting that most folks found dull. She was fascinated by the number of historical news stories that had been broken by seemingly mundane details. A hotel receipt left in a pocket at the dry cleaner. Call records to the Chinese take-out place blocks from a secret love nest. The more obscure the detail, the more satisfying the payoff if it succeeded in unraveling a web of obfuscation.

Jason was sitting with his elbow on the table and his chin resting in the palm of his hand. He seemed to be dozing off repeatedly, his arm sliding off the corner of the table, causing his head to bob down just enough that it would jolt him awake. When it happened again, his eyes popped open to see Alex chuckling at him.

"I'm about ready to call it a night too," Alex said as Jason looked around, disoriented from his catnaps. "Carley, are you coming or do you want to stick around?"

"Can I? I figured I'd have to leave when you did. I probably shouldn't even be here in the first place."

"No, you probably shouldn't be," Alex admitted. "But you're clearly better at this part of the job than I am. I can leave you a key though. I doubt anyone will be coming by at this hour."

Carley checked her watch. After all the late nights the last few months, and the subsequent arguments with Luke, she should probably go home, but...

"Yeah," she said as Alex and Jason got their things together. "I think I'll keep digging for a little longer. I just have this *feeling* that something is in here."

"Suit yourself," Alex said as they headed out the door.

27.

THE PAPER WAS LYING in the driveway when Luke walked outside. Even after all these years in the business, he still got a charge out of seeing his stories on the front page. Money and power are one thing, liquor is another, but for a dyed-in-the-wool reporter, a byline under a breaking news headline is the one true high. This morning, that buzz was dovetailed with a touch of apprehension, partly because he wasn't completely behind the story as written, but mostly due to something he'd added to the piece after Carley approved it.

Luke scanned the next page til he found the sentence in question.

"Though it appears Taylor and Mealy were acting alone, the investigation is ongoing, and police continue to follow credible leads."

If the Chief of Police *had* been leaning on them to provide a sense of closure he wouldn't be happy with Luke's last-minute editorial footnote. His editor-in-chief was likely to be unhappy as well. It was only a matter of time before he got an angry call from one of them.

He was heading inside when the phone began to ring.

⌐∽

Carley woke with a start.

Her cell phone was ringing.

She looked around in confusion, struggling to determine why half her vision had gone white. Then she reached a hand up to her forehead and pulled away a sheet of paper that had stuck to her face with dried drool. She had of course stayed in the lab all night, staring at the papers and going through emails and documents on the seized laptops, until her vision grew fuzzy and she set her head on the table, just for a moment, and wound up sleeping through the night.

"Hello?" she said into her phone once she'd extricated it from the pile of documents.

"It's me," Luke said. "Where are you?"

She sat up, looking around the room and trying to think of a way to avoid telling him she had done precisely the thing he'd asked her not to do. Not that either of them would have been surprised by that these days.

"I'm still here," she admitted.

Her confession was met by silence.

"Are you mad?" she asked defensively.

"No, sorry, I was just looking for my camera. I figured you wouldn't stop digging til you found something."

"Why do you want your camera?"

"I just got a call from Alan Greenwood's assistant-"

"Oh, is this the famous coffee expert *Kim?*"

"Now that you mention it, no. This was a guy. I hope Greenwood didn't let her go, she seemed nice-"

"What was the call about?" Carley interrupted.

"Greenwood invited me out for a final interview and tour of the facility now that it's come online. I'm supposed to meet him there at noon. I asked if it was all right if I took some pictures to go along with the story. Does that sound OK?"

"That's a good idea," Carley said as she rubbed her eyes sleepily. "We could stand to have a few pictures of the facility on file."

The door behind her opened and she swiveled around in her chair to see Jason and Alex walking in with a drink carrier.

"See," Alex said to Jason as she handed Carley a coffee. "I *told* you she'd still be here."

"Thanks," Carley said as she took the coffee, noticing the *Cryptic Grindings* logo on the side of the cup. "Speak of the devil-"

"What devil?" Luke asked.

"Nothing. Alex and Jason just got here. Good luck out there today. Try not to piss him off this time," Carley said as she inhaled the aroma from her coffee.

"I'll do my best. Speaking of which, I'd better get back to the camera search if I don't want to keep him waiting."

"I'll talk to you later, Luke," Carley said. She hung up the phone and took a sip of her coffee. "Damn," she murmured, pointing to the cup of coffee. "This is delicious."

"Right?" Alex said as she flipped on the TV, letting the muted morning news play in the background as she sat down.

"Finding anything interesting?" Jason asked.

"Actually, yeah," Carley replied. "There are a few emails between Larson and Florquist, and Mealy and someone else that I wanted to go over with you."

"Fire away," Jason said.

Sunlight glinted off the razor wire that ran along the fencing. Compared to the openly hostile protection Diane Haubert and company had provided for the generating station and mine, Luke was surprised how lax the security at The Greenwood Project appeared to be. Now that it was online, he expected the place to me clamped down tighter than it had been on his previous visit, but if anything, security measures appeared to have slid even further. The guard booth was unmanned this time. Adding to the curious scene, the gate was wide open as well.

Luke paused at the entrance, debating whether or not to wait here or continue on inside, then he stepped on the gas and pulled the Cadillac through the gate. Greenwood had said the plant would run on minimal manpower. Apparently the security guard had been one of the first people to go once the automation ramped up.

Gravel crunched under the tires as Luke drove into the complex, making his way through row after row of glimmering solar panels. The drive was much the same as on his previous visit, only now a low, steady hum hung in the air as the longhorns barreled forward, noonday sun overhead, red bluffs in the distance, and the hulking mass of the main building growing in size as he neared the far corner of the facility.

The building looked much the same as well, the only difference being a greater density of conduit and cables running in and out of the massive structure that sat poised over the property like an enormous concrete and steel spider, its zigzagging stairways and catwalks looming over the cracked, sunbaked ground below.

Luke parked the Cadillac at the base of one of the staircases, slinging his camera over his shoulder as he got out and looked around.

Alan Greenwood's signature electric car was nowhere in sight.

"Take me through this slowly," Alex said. "This is not my area of expertise. I'm more of a 'which way did the blood splatter' kind of girl."

"OK," Carley said. "I was going through some of the emails from Buck Florquist's computer. He was the driver who burned alive in front of that family out on State Road 170, right?"

"Yeah. The guy from outside Durango."

"Well, in addition to a handful of messages to Jeff Larson, he was in frequent contact with an email account with the address info@sandstonepower.com," Carley said as she pulled up a list of emails.

"And who was that address for?" Jason asked.

"I don't know, the account name just comes up as 'Sandstone.'"

"What were those emails about exactly?" Alex asked.

"I'm no energy industry expert, but it looks like it was some sort of feasibility analysis for taking the generating station private after the solar project came online. Florquist was involved in much of the same research years ago when Larson and his family were upgrading their systems to increase production for Farmington. Once the city became energy independent, it seems Sandstone was planning to take over and sell the power to Bloomfield and other communities in the region."

"Do we know who owns 'Sandstone?'" Alex asked.

"Unfortunately, no. As Luke has pointed out, that seems to be how these businesses work. One entity owns another, which then owns another. You never really know *who* gets to deposit the checks in their account. That's one of the primary questions I was trying to answer. Which is where the ownership breakdown of the solar project comes in. Are you familiar with the way Greenwood's project was set up?"

"Not really. I've read a few of the articles you guys have run, but I don't have all that much background. Plus, it seemed sort of…"

"Boring as hell?"

"Yeah," Alex admitted. "I mean, Luke's articles were interesting, but the topic just wasn't on my radar until recently."

"Trust me, I know. I was the one who had to keep telling him to write that stuff. It wasn't until people started burning to death that things got interesting."

When he got tired of waiting, Luke began poking around the building. He tested the sliding metals doors, but they were locked. He assumed that meant Greenwood was still on his way, rather than out in the sea of solar panels, buzzing around in his fancy golf cart.

A transient noise from above caught his attention. He peered up into the blinding light. Out here in the height of the midday heat, it could have been anything. A bird landing on the walkways above, an unseen technician checking the equipment, or, most likely, simply the metal of the new structure twisting and popping as it settled into place in the relentless heat.

Luke stepped out from the shade, shielding his eyes as he again peered up into the rat's nest of crisscrossing metal walkways. He should have brought his sunglasses. What had ever happened to them? Likely lost in the wreckage of his dearly departed Mustang.

It was just about impossible to see *anything* out here with the sun directly overhead. When you threw in the surroundings, with every inch covered in solar panels, seeing anything above eye level was nearly impossible. Luke squinted, trying his best to scan the overhead walkways in the blinding light.

Another noise, one sounding remarkably like a footstep, reverberated from somewhere high up above.

Luke looked at his watch. It was now 12:15. He listened for the sound of tires on gravel in the distance. Finally, he approached the nearest staircase and began to climb.

~

"The ownership structure of The Greenwood Project," Alex said. "Can you give me the CliffsNotes explanation?"

"In a nutshell, Alan Greenwood co-owns the solar facility with another investment group: Electron Holdings. I forget the exact percentages, but it's something like 60/40, with Greenwood owning the larger percentage, and things written out in all sorts of weird legalese, so that in exchange for the city kicking in ten percent of the final construction cost, in 25 years, Greenwood transfers his ownership stake, in total, over to the city."

Jason piped in, "And since the production exceeds the city's needs, that makes Farmington one of the first cities in the country to be powered by 100 percent renewable electricity. In twenty-five years, it will then be energy independent to boot."

"In the meantime, just like with Sandstone, in exchange for funding their portion of the construction, the other investment group has final say over where and how the surplus power from the facility is sold to communities and customers outside the city limits."

"What if something were to happen to Greenwood before the 25 years is up?" Alex asked. "I'm thinking of the attempt on his life. That has to play into this somehow."

"I'm fairly certain it does. Unless Greenwood found a way around it, if something were to happen to him, Electron Holdings has the right to purchase his shares outright, and the eventual hand-off to the city would be off the table. "

"That's a pretty good motive for a rogue investor," Jason observed.

"Any idea who heads up Electron Holdings?" Alex asked.

"Another unknown," Carley said. "But I'm getting closer."

"*Please* tell me it involves something sexy, like more of those emails."

"You're in luck," Carley said as she opened another laptop. "This is one of the computers from Bill Mealy's home. He exchanged a number of messages with the email address contact@electronholdings.com, which again has no name attached to it. No mailing address. No phone number. Just a web domain with a generic placeholder page set up. Exactly the same as for Sandstone Power. So that got me thinking about ICANN and my old job at *The Aztec Review*."

"What is ICANN?" Alex asked.

"They track and follow the information connected with various web domains, Jason explained. "If you buy a URL and set up a website, it will list the information of the company or person who registered that address."

"When I ran *The Aztec Review*, I used to get emails all the time asking me to check the WHOIS data for the paper's website," Carley explained. "I ignored it for years, then one day I finally took a moment to check the information they'd been wanting me to update, and realized the ICANN data still listed my father's home address and phone number from when he'd first bought the URL in 1997."

"Let's bring this back around," Alex said, drawing a circle in the air with her finger. "What did you find out?"

When he got to the building's forth level, Luke removed the cap from his camera and raised the viewfinder to his eye. It took a moment to find the right settings so the image wouldn't end up being totally blown out.

He scanned the surrounding landscape through the viewfinder, marveling, not for the first time, at what a vast facility Greenwood had constructed. Ben Gerritt's dubious complex in Chokecherry Canyon had been big, but the solar project dwarfed it.

Luke took a few more shots of the glimmering panels. Then he lowered the camera and looked down at his little Boss Hogg car parked far below.

He was pretty high up.

The metal catwalks for the third and second levels crisscrossed beneath him.

Luke raised the camera again, and was just framing a shot looking down through the intersecting steelwork, when he heard the distinct sound of footsteps overhead, and looked up to see a figure crossing the highest catwalk above him. Luke hadn't seen Greenwood's car since he'd arrived, but for all he knew, the weirdo had flown out here with a jetpack or something. Who else would it be? It wasn't getting any easier to see out here as the sun climbed higher in the sky, but as the first foot set down on the stairs, Luke was able to make out what appeared to be very nice fabric on the pantleg. This wasn't some worker in jeans or canvas Carhartts, whoever this was, he was wearing a suit. That greatly reduced the list of likely arrivals.

Luke stood off to the side, just out of the direct line of sight from the stairs. He held his camera at the ready, aiming to get a candid snapshot of Alan Greenwood descending the stairs before he gave the final tour of his latest daydream brought to life.

"The websites in question were sandstonepower.com and electron-holdings.com," Carley said. "When I punched in Sandstone's URL, the information came back with this mailing address."

She pointed to the screen, which read: 3005 Northridge Drive, Farmington, NM.

"When I typed in Electron Holdings' can you guess what happened?"

"The same information came up," Jason said.

"Exactly," Carley replied. "3005 Northridge Drive in Farmington"

Alex leaned forward, studying the display. "What's at that location?"

"It's an office building, owned by someone with *one more* URL also registered to that address."

"And what website is that?" Jason asked.

"It's a campaign page."

Alex raised an eyebrow. "For whom?"

The gun caught him by surprise.

He almost missed it in the glare, but a split second before Luke's eyes adjusted to the light, a mirrored flare reflected back from the weapon's barrel. When the new arrival reached the bottom of the stairs and turned to face him, it wasn't Alan Greenwood, but-

"*Tim Givens,*" Luke murmured.

The name echoed in his head as he looked on in confusion. His mind was a jumble. Yet somehow, something about the councilman's presence suddenly made complete sense. Like a puzzle piece falling neatly into place.

Luke pressed the shutter release on his camera, snapping a picture of Tim Givens walking toward him, gun in hand.

"Surprised?" Givens asked. "Please, take as many pictures as you like. I'll just dispose of them after…"

"After what?"

"Come on, Luke," Givens said as he raised the gun in his hand. "I think you know where this is going."

Luke pivoted, ready to run, but changing his tactic at the final moment. If he sprinted the length of walkway to the stairs, Givens would have that much distance to take him down. Instead, Luke twisted around, planting his hands on the railing behind him and swinging his legs up and over the bar before plunging out of sight. His stomach hung in his throat as he waited to see if he'd misjudged the distance between the fourth and third levels.

He crashed down on the metal walkway below, landing hard on his feet and tumbling to the side. The lens on the camera crunched as his full body weight crashed down on top of it.

He could only hope the camera's memory was intact.

"Jesus, Luke," Givens called down to him. "You could get yourself *killed* doing stunts like that."

Luke struggled to his feet, staggering towards a metal doorway on the outside of the concrete building. He ducked into the alcove and tested the door's handle.

Locked.

He pressed his back against the metal as he studied the silhouette on the catwalk above, watching closely as Givens patiently made his way to the next set of stairs, which would bring him down to the third level.

"Don't worry, this will be over soon enough," Givens said. "Normally, I'd have Bill Mealy or Dub Taylor handle this kind of thing for me, but your detective friend went and shot Mealy. And unfortunately, I thought I no longer needed Taylor's services."

More pieces were fitting together in Luke's head.

"I thought for sure you'd believe those two were working alone," Givens said. "That you'd take Taylor's suicide at face value, see it as a sign that the killings were over. The cops bought it, or they wanted to at least. Then I get up this morning, read the front-page story in *The Times*, and realize you're just not gonna drop this and let things get back to normal, are you?"

Luke knew what Givens was going to say next…

"Police continue to follow credible leads?" Givens exclaimed. "Now, why in the hell did you have to end with that, Luke? If you'd simply wrapped it up neatly, neither of us would be here now. But you just had to go and get cute, didn't you?"

The Councilman had reached the top of the stairs. Luke knew Givens would have his weapon at the ready, that this time, he'd come out shooting. His eyes went to the rail ten feet from the building. He couldn't remember where exactly the next walkway fell, he *thought* it ran perpendicular to where he was standing now, but he didn't want to get this wrong.

Givens started down the stairs.

It was now or never.

Luke ran for the edge, once more jumping over the rail and kicking off from the bar as he launched himself into the air.

The moment he looked down, he knew his aim had been off.

He was going to miss the next walkway by at least a foot. Beneath the catwalk sat the shimmering, angled surface of a solar panel. Luke threw his arm out to the side. His best hope was to grab the next guardrail and hold on tight. Maybe he'd be able to catch himself, but without question, it was going to hurt like hell.

Trying to correct his fall was his second mistake.

His hand smashed down on the railing *hard*, but he managed to hold on long enough for the weight of his body to swing down, smashing him into the side of the walkway. Something in his shoulder twisted and popped like a chicken bone. Luke hollered in pain and let go, beginning his second descent, which ended just as painfully as the first.

He crashed down on the solar panel. The surface buckled beneath him, splintering out in a blast pattern of shattered glass, which grew increasingly chaotic as Givens fired down on him. Bullets tore into the panel as Luke tumbled out of control down its face, clawing for something, *anything* to grab ahold of. But it was no use, and just as well, as stopping his fall would only slice up his hands and give the councilman a clean shot at him. Instead, he went limp and gave in to gravity, flailing until he ran out of solar panel and pinwheeled off the edge toward the hard desert floor. He smashed down, stunned but all too aware that he had to get to cover.

Gunshots rang out as bullets blasted dirt clods up from the cracked ground around him. It wasn't until Luke managed to pull himself under the corner of the panel –gasping and sputtering in pain – that the gunfire ended.

"You're telling me Givens is behind the company that's acquiring the generating station," Alex began. "While *also* heading up the investment group that's backing the solar project's minority shares?"

Carley nodded. "Meaning that if something happens to Greenwood before he turns control over to the city, Givens, through his investment group, can acquire Greenwood's shares and nix the deal."

"Which is why he sent Mealy to get rid of Greenwood that night," Jason said.

"That didn't work out as planned," Alex mused. "But it's just a matter of time. He's got, what, a twenty-five year window to make that happen?"

"In the simplest terms, he's pretended to be a renewable energy skeptic, while using shell companies to hand himself control of virtually *all* electric production in the region."

"If we're right, then anyone who was targeted and survived is still in danger," Alex said. "Where is Luke at the moment?"

Carley was already punching his number into her phone. "He's supposed to be meeting Greenwood at the solar project *right now!*"

Alex shook her head. "I don't think so." She pointed to the TV on the other side of the room, where the broadcast showed Alan Greenwood sitting with a very serious looking man in a dark suit. Jason reached for the remote and turned up the volume.

The news anchor's voice blared through the speaker:

"Businessman Alan Greenwood is in Santa Fe this morning, meeting with the governor to discuss the construction of additional solar projects throughout the state."

"If Greenwood is in Santa Fe, who is Luke meeting at the plant?" Jason asked.

"I've got a pretty good guess!" Alex shouted as she ran for the door.

If his ankle wasn't broken, it was sure as hell fractured.

Luke pulled his phone from his pocket and tried to call Calvin Mann.

The call wouldn't go through.

He looked at the screen. No service.

Just for the hell of it, he tried Alex's phone. Of course, that didn't work either.

He knew the safety provided by the solar panel would be short-lived. His car was a good distance away. The chances of getting to it unscathed were zero.

His best bet was to get as far from the main building as possible, lose himself in the sea of solar panels, and hope to hell he could evade Givens long enough to circle back to his car, where he'd left the keys in the ignition. How he would do that with a fucked up ankle was another matter.

Bam!

A bullet ripped into a nearby panel. Fortunately, Givens was too far away to get a close bead on Luke from where he was standing. If the councilman kept it up however, someone would undoubtedly be arriving at the facility to figure out why so many brand-new solar panels were going offline.

Luke shielded his eyes and peered out towards the building. Givens had stopped shooting and was running through the maze of metal walkways, making his way down to ground level.

∽

Alex smashed the accelerator to the car's floorboards as she raced out of town to the solar project.

She again dialed Luke's number.

Again, the call went straight to voicemail.

She threw her phone on the passenger seat.

There was no time to leave him a message. If she didn't get there soon, he was a dead man.

∽

Luke limped among the panels. So far, despite his ankle, and whatever he'd done to his shoulder, he was keeping ahead of Givens. Hopefully that would continue. He adjusted his course continually as he stumbled among the towering panels, weaving back and forth in a crisscrossing pattern, well aware of the fact that his next run-in with Tim Givens would likely be his last.

The sun was beating down on the top of his head. Luke squinted at his feet as he walked, following the tiny circle of his own shadow. He fell against the base of the nearest panel – the pain in his ankle radiating up his leg – and heard a sound a short distance behind.

Tim Givens was gaining on him.

Alex arrived to find the security booth empty and the main gate wide open. She sailed through the entrance, racing down a stretch of gravel road, and slammed on the brakes when she noticed tire marks turning left onto a side route. She backed up and followed suit.

When a concrete and steel structure emerged with Luke's loaner Cadillac parked at its the base, she knew she'd arrived at her destination. She parked next to Luke's ride and started looking around.

A vulture circled overhead.

Otherwise, there were no visible signs of life.

Alex approached the building, tested the doors, but found each of them locked. She stepped away from the structure, raising a hand to shield her eyes as she scanned the walkways overhead.

Finally, she walked over to Luke's car, and had just spotted the pink rabbit's foot keychain dangling from the ignition, when she heard the crack of a gunshot somewhere in the distance. She whipped her head around, seeing nothing but light reflections and solar panels in every direction.

Another shot rang out.

A panel to the left of Luke's head exploded in a cloud of splintered glass. He dove for cover, ducking behind a wide, metal pole at the base of the nearest panel. He pressed his spine against the steel, pulling his arms in close to his body as he did his best to disappear amongst the equipment. He held his breath, straining his ears to determine where the shot had come from.

After several long moments, a movement caught his eye. He watched and waited, until finally, Tim Givens emerged on a narrow maintenance path that ran amongst the panels.

No sooner did Luke see him, then the councilman turned in his direction and squeezed off a shot.

The roar of a car engine filled the air.

The longhorns raced down the narrow stretch running between the panels, giving Alex the point of view a steer might enjoy at the annual running of the bulls.

Givens was standing in the middle of the path, firing to the side. He spun around at the sound of the Cadillac's engine, taking aim at the approaching car, and managing to get off two shots. The first went wide. The second took off the tip of the right horn.

Alex hit the gas and clenched the wheel, steering the car right for him. The left horn, still sharp and true, tore into Tim Givens' stomach as the Cadillac went out of control, smashing into row after row of panels. Alex stomped on the brakes, her stomach dropping as they appeared to do nothing. After a horrified split second, she mashed the emergency brake down, and the heavy car went into a slide, taking down three more panels before it came to a stop.

Alex staggered out of the car to take in the damage. The Cadillac was thoroughly torn up. She didn't know anything about solar equipment, but she could practically hear cash registers going off in her head as she assessed the damage.

Tim Givens was sprawled across the hood. Alex felt for a pulse and found one, but he was in bad shape, thoroughly gored by the Cadillac even before the car had pinballed off of Alan Greenwood's dream project.

Luke stumbled out from amongst the panels, his left arm hanging loose at his side, a smashed camera slung over his shoulder.

He winced as he caught sight of the carnage. "Is he alive?"

"Barely."

"How did you know I was here?"

"Your girlfriend," Alex said as she checked her phone. No service. "Carley fit all the pieces together. I'll explain it to you shortly, but if we want this dirt bag to stand trial, I need to get back to my car and radio for an ambulance. There's no phone service out here."

"I know," Luke moaned. "That's another lesson I learned the hard way."

28.

LUKE SAT NEXT TO Carley in the press area for Alan Greenwood's latest public event, which Greenwood had hastily organized the night before, shortly after learning of everything that had gone down while he was in Santa Fe.

Luke snuck a couple of marshmallow peanuts from the snack bag he'd tucked into his sling, and glanced over at an older gentleman reading *The Daily Times* a few seats away. He got that familiar buzz in his stomach when he saw the photo he'd taken of Tim Givens, gun in hand, along with his cover story.

"A picture is worth a thousand words," Carley said when she saw where Luke was looking.

"I'm just glad it survived after the abuse that camera endured," Luke replied. "They could always read the story," Carley whispered as the lights began to dim.

"Yeah," Luke conceded. "But you know how people are, they need that one indelible image before they'll take in the facts."

"That's fine with me, whatever it takes, just as long as they get it from *our* paper-" Alan Greenwood, no longer in a wheelchair, emerged from behind a curtain. He looked significantly stronger as he walked up to the lectern, adjusted the microphone, and took a deep breath.

Luke reach over with his good arm and tapped Carley on the leg.

"Ladies and gentlemen," Greenwood began. "You may see me as a businessman, but I'm really just a dreamer. Which is why the events of the last twenty-four hours have been so shocking for me. When I set out to build The Greenwood Project I had but one vision. To one day give the people of Farmington true energy independence. Though I felt it was necessary to work with outside business partnerships, it seems, unfortunately, that an anonymous investor spearheading that group harbored more sinister intentions. Fortunately, that individual has been apprehended and will be dealt with."

The audience applauded.

"Which brings me to the purpose of today's event. Originally, I planned to wait a number of years before handing over control of the project, but I have other dreams to make a reality. And, having seen the corrupting allure inherent in the way I co-financed this venture, I've decided to move up my original timeline."

Greenwood raised an ornate, oversized document above his head.

"Rather than waiting twenty years to turn the Greenwood Solar Project over to the city, with this document, I am hereby granting ownership of The Greenwood Project, *full* ownership of The Greenwood Project, to the people of Farmington *today.*"

Camera flashes went off as the audience applauded uproariously.

When the commotion finally died down, Luke raised his hand and made eye contact with Greenwood, who squinted subtly, wondering perhaps if calling on Luke was a wise move. Finally, he relented, pointing to the man who had saved his life.

"Yes, Mr. Murphy. You have a question?"

"I do. You said you're ready to move on to something new."

"I am."

"Can you give us some idea of what that might be?"

"The stars are the limit as they say, so I'm thinking of something to do with… space," Greenwood announced dramatically before walking off stage.

The audience whistled and applauded as Luke nodded his head uncertainly.

"*Space?*" he mouthed to Carley.

That would be interesting.

⌒

Alex and Calvin were waiting for them in the reception area.

"I knew they shouldn't have reassigned me so soon," Calvin said, noting Luke's sling as they shook hands.

"No worries," Luke replied. "That's where Detective Spencer comes in."

"Next time we'll be more cautious," Alex said.

"Please, let's hope there is no next time. I got beat up more than enough on this story."

"Well, let's not say anything rash," Carley interjected. "I don't necessarily want my star reporter dislocating his shoulder and dodging bullets for *every* story, but a little extreme reporting every six to twelve months does wonders for daily circulation."

Luke gave his law enforcement friends a look of apprehension. "You see what I'm dealing with here? *Cold-blooded.*"

"She had your back. Don't let her fool you," Alex said. "Carley, next time we're bringing you in from the get-go. This guy's good for stunt work, but that deep dive you did *cracked* this one."

"Didn't I tell you she was good at that boring stuff?" Luke interjected as his phone began to ring. He ducked to the side to answer it.

"I've been thinking about the newspaper business and law enforcement," Carley mused. "There's definitely some overlap in the way we do things."

"Like what?" Alex asked.

"Well, for starters, we're always on deadline, and we never know what's coming up next."

"*And* we often see the very best and the very worst in people."

"That's true!" Carley said. "We've got more in common than I thought."

"Who was that?" Alex asked Luke as he walked back to the group.

"Nick at the garage," he replied warily as he checked his watch. "He said to meet him there at noon. He has a new car for me."

"Why do you look so worried?" Alex asked.

"Are you nervous after what happened the last time someone told you to meet them someplace at noon?" Calvin asked.

"No. I'm scared he might actually have a car for me! God only knows what he's got in store for me this time!"

Carley smiled at Alex knowingly. "Come on," she said as she headed for the exit. "There's only one way to find out. I'll drive you."

The Cadillac looked pretty sad parked in front of Nick's Auto Repair. One horn was broken in half, while the other was pulled forward and caked with dried blood. The front grill was crunched in. The entire passenger-side was scraped and smashed from front to back. The windshield was a spider's web of shattered glass.

"Boy, Alex really did a number on that, didn't she?"

"Yeah," Nick said to Luke sadly. "That's one way of putting it."

"In her defense, you did say the horns would be a good way of running someone through."

"I didn't think anyone should actually *do it* though."

"Who ended up paying for the damage?" Carley asked. "Our insurance or the Farmington PD's?"

"They're still sorting that out between them."

"Any luck finding a new set of horns?" Luke asked.

Nick raised a hand in the air. "Honestly, I'd rather not talk about the Cadillac just yet."

"Gotcha. So, what have you got for me? Remember my parameters. No tacos. Nothing silly."

Nick walked over and hit the button on the garage door.

Luke shot Carley another wary look as the door began rolling up slowly, revealing from the ground up: a set of brand-new black tires, a shiny chrome bumper, and a gleaming red hood. By the time he could see the windshield, Luke knew exactly what he was looking at. A mint condition, impeccably detailed, 1968 Mustang convertible.

"What do you think?" Nick asked.

Luke's mouth hung open.

Carley nudged him with her elbow. "Look at the license plate."

The front plate read: "PAGE ONE"

"This is a loaner?" Luke asked incredulously.

"No man, this is *yours*."

"I thought my car was totaled?"

"Oh, yeah, *that* car was totaled," Nick said in that amused tone Luke had come to associate with automotive calamity. "That was *totaled* totaled. This baby on the other hand is better than brand new. Fully restored. Same year. Same model. Top to bottom restoration. Brand new coat of red paint. It's a beauty if I do say so myself."

"But, where did it come from?"

Nick pointed to Carley. "Your lady bought it for you."

Carley shrugged. "The Puzzlebox guys gave me that bonus. We surpassed every target they set for us, and honestly half of that was due to your coverage of the Givens crime spree."

"This is too much," Luke protested.

"Trust me, Luke, I've treated myself to one or two indulgences as well. It was a *very* nice bonus. Besides, I couldn't take much more of that Cadillac, even before Alex started mowing people down with it." She reached into her pocket and pulled out a set of keys, which she placed in his hand as she gave him a kiss. "Why don't we take it for a spin?" "OK," Luke said as he got into the driver's seat. "If you insist."

"Nick, thanks for everything," Carley said as she walked around to the passenger side and opened the door. "With any luck, we'll make it a week before he's back in here for repairs."

"Shouldn't we head back to the office and file one last story on The Greenwood Project?" Luke asked as he started the car.

"With all due respect, I am sick to *death* of Alan Greenwood, Tim Givens, and anything else to do with that damn solar project," Carley said as she reached for the radio and cranked up the volume. "The hell with the story, I want to see what this new car of yours can do!"

"OK then," Luke said as he gunned the engine and pulled out of the garage. "You're the boss!"

GET THE VERY FIRST
BRICK RANSOM STORY FOR FREE

Building a relationship with my readers is one of the most exciting parts of my writing career. I occasionally send newsletters with information on upcoming releases, special offers, and other exclusive content, like the BRICK RANSOM story I'm offering at the moment.

To get the story and see how it all began, please sign up at
http://www.mikeattebery.com

DID YOU ENJOY THIS BOOK?
YOU CAN MAKE A HUGE DIFFERENCE.

Reviews are the most powerful tools in my utility belt when it comes to getting attention for my writing. As an indie author, resources for advertising and media exposure are limited, fortunately, word of mouth is every bit as effective.

The support of readers means the world to me.

Honest reviews of my books are invaluable in bringing them to the attention of other readers. Word of mouth is my greatest weapon!

If you enjoyed this book, I would be extremely grateful if you could take a moment and leave a review.

THANK YOU VERY MUCH FOR YOUR SUPPORT.

ABOUT THE AUTHOR

Mike Attebery is the author of seven novels, including Chokecherry Canyon, Rosé in Saint Tropez, and the Brick Ransom thrillers Seattle On Ice, Bloody Pulp, and Billionaires Bullets Exploding Monkeys. Mike lives with his family on an island off the coast of Washington State, where he is currently at work on a new four book series.

You can find Mike online at:
www.facebook.com/AtteberyBooks/
on twitter at @Mikeattebery
and on his website http://www.mikeattebery.com